DREAD
A·N·D
WATER

DREAD AND WATER

DOUGLAS CLARK

PERENNIAL LIBRARY
Harper & Row, Publishers
New York, Cambridge, Philadelphia, San Francisco
London, Mexico City, São Paulo, Sydney

First PERENNIAL LIBRARY edition published 1984.

LIBRARY OF CONGRESS CATALOG CARD NUMBER: 83-48336

ISBN 0-06-080688-5

84 85 86 87 88 10 9 8 7 6 5 4 3 2 1

Chapter 1

"CAN ANYBODY GIVE me a good reason why doctors of philosophy, particularly those with a bent towards the sciences and scientific research, should be dedicated mountaineers?" asked Detective Superintendent George Masters.

Detective Sergeant Brant, who was driving, said: "Perhaps they like the good, clean, mountain air after mucking about in labs all their working lives. Terrible smells in labs sometimes. You must remember sulphuretted hydrogen and how it stinks."

"We don't want any of your schoolboy reminiscences," said DI Green. "Even when I went to school there were fume chambers. Just because you made bad-egg gas to stink the place out, it doesn't mean that professional egg-heads inflict the same punishment on themselves."

"Modern physical sciences don't create smells," said Masters quietly. "They give you shocks instead."

"Apart from which," said Detective Sergeant Hill, sitting in the front passenger seat, "modern labs are air-conditioned and air-purified. They shove the air through scrubbers to clean it up."

Green was sitting in the—to him—safe nearside back seat. His usual position in the car; always tacitly left for him by Masters who, recognising Green's apprehension on the road, carefully contrived to board the vehicle last. The traffic on the road west out of London was not heavy at this time on a Sunday afternoon: that indeterminate time about half past three on a dry, cold, grey Sunday in early April when Easter has passed by almost unnoticed by humans and without rousing the countryside to spring activity. So Green was not too fearful, but scarcely cheerful at being dragged out on a Sunday.

"I'm feeling bright," he said lugubriously. "I didn't miss that remark about modern science giving people shocks. Has it given us one?"

"I'm afraid so."

"All those doctors of philosophy you were going on about?"

Masters nodded.

"Murder?"

It was almost an unnecessary question because all four of them rarely worked together these days on anything less. But it was not quite unnecessary this time.

"Maybe. Maybe three or more murders. We've got to decide for ourselves."

"And then investigate?"

"Can you see us avoiding it?"

Green grunted and took a Kensitas from a badly crumpled packet. Good detective as he was, Masters had never been able to discover why Green's cigarette packets were always crumpled. They must have been pristine when bought, but they never survived for long in their original condition.

"No. We'll be stuck with it." Green sucked his top partial denture in to signify disapproval before mouthing his cigarette. "But you mentioned mountaineering. Have we got to start climbing bloody great crags?"

"I think not. I say that because all the men we're interested in fell to the bottom of them. That's why we're interested."

"All leading scientists?" asked Hill.

"Government employees at Pottersby Research Centre."

"Down in Berkshire?"

"That's it."

The car purred on, clearing London proper and entering the outskirts. The wayside trees were still bare. Here and there in gardens the pink of flowering almond blossom gave fragile promise of better things to come while carpeting the ground with petals. The daffodils, perversely doing well despite the weather, clumped gold with green, claiming the right of primogeniture.

"We'd better have it all," said Green. "So's we don't have to speculate in the dark."

Masters was filling his pipe with Warlock Flake. He said:

6

"Your memory's better than mine," which was partly true in that Green could remember facts like a music hall memory-man, where Masters could cast back and do mental fishing, "so you'll probably recall reading in the newspapers about two fatal accidents to scientists who were climbing."

"Two?" asked Green. "I can remember one. Even his name. Redruth. But it must have been all of six months ago."

"Last October," agreed Masters, "and you're quite correct. Dr Philip Redruth. The other, last March—that is, a year ago—involved Dr Stanley Silk."

"D'you mean to say that now, after intervals of six months and a year, somebody has suggested those two might have been murdered?"

"Only because there's been a third one. This morning in North Wales. He wasn't dead when we left the Yard, but he was so close to it that he's probably gone by now."

"All from Pottersby, you said?" asked Green.

"More than that. All from the same section at Pottersby."

"Ah!" breathed Green. "Now I get it. The long arm of coincidence has killed three boffins in precisely the same way, so the long arm of the law has been alerted to discover the whys and wherefores."

"Right on the button," said Masters. "That's why I said I didn't know whether there had been three or more murders, or none at all. Coincidence has been mentioned. Professionally we mistrust coincidences—although they're naturally occurring phenomena. But we make use of them, as now, when we are using one to arouse a suspicion within ourselves which will feed on the lack of trust we place in the very coincidence that has alerted us."

"Is that the end of the lecture?" asked Green, "because if so, I'd like to know where those three copped it. All in North Wales?"

"Just this last one—Clive Mailer—in Snowdonia. Redruth on Ben Nevis and Silk in the Lake District."

"Oughtn't we to be going up to Wales? Just in case this chap Mailer does recover enough to mutter a few words?"

"That's been taken care of. There's a relay of intelligent jacks

7

standing by with tape recorders and laryngophones as well as notebooks."

"You mean they've got mikes strapped to the throttle box of a dying man?"

"He's concussed—unconscious. He doesn't know; and it could be the means of saving other lives."

Green grimaced. "Some hope! All they'll get from that'll be a death rattle."

"Pottersby itself is the common factor in all three deaths," said Masters. "It seems to me a safe bet that any skullduggery involved emanated from there—or rather from one or more of its personnel. So that's where we should look first."

The car was approaching Reading, the afternoon growing duller as they went, although there were still several hours of British Summertime daylight to come.

"I suppose we'll be faced with hundreds of forgetful professors," moaned Green. "Every one so immersed in some project as to have no time to notice anything else. And if by some chance they did notice anything, they'd have forgotten it the next day. So we're in for a rum time."

"Could be," agreed Masters. "There's very little else I know. Redruth was climbing solo on a pretty easy pitch. . . ."

"Now we get the jargon," interrupted Green. "Anybody know what abseil means?"

The others ignored him. "Climbing solo?" asked Hill. "That's a bit risky. I thought nobody ever did that."

"Silk was roped to a partner—a novice," said Masters.

"Did he cop it? The partner, I mean."

"Fortunately not. I wasn't told how he managed to escape."

"And Mailer?"

"Alone again. I was told his protection failed—whatever that may mean."

"Expanding nuts," said Green. "They shove 'em into cracks and crevices; expand them to a tight fit and then belay themselves. . . ."

"Now who's producing the jargon?" asked Brant. "From the sound of it, you know what it's all about."

8

"Not me. And watch your speed, Sergeant. The limit's forty on the Reading by-pass."

Brant slowed slightly.

"If none of us knows anything about mountaineering," said Masters, "let us hope that the investigation will not rely solely on a working knowledge of climbing techniques."

"If it doesn't do that," said Green, "among that lot of suspects it'll depend on our being familiar with the second law of thermodynamics. I don't know which will be worse."

"It must be the weather," said Hill. "Anybody would think, listening to the conversation in this car, that we'd never been out on a case before, let alone solved one. OK. So we've had our failures—but no more than anybody else and far fewer than most —except, perhaps, Sherlock Holmes."

"You're like an old woman talking when her belly's full of buttermilk," sneered Green. "Well done, our side! We're frightfully keen on being keen on cricket!"

"Stow it," said Masters. "Both of you. As an onlooker I can safely say you're both as bad as each other when it comes to chalking up success. And don't tell me I'm even worse. I know I am, and I revel in it. If I can't be successful most of the time, I don't want to play. Success is sweet to me; and the harder the problem, the greater the success."

"Honesty is the best policy," said Green. "It'll get you anywhere—and I don't think! This show we're heading for is going to be a headache. I can feel it in my water."

Pottersby village was picturesque. Even in the fading light of a dull day the timbered cottages and thatched roofs argued picture postcards. Though nominally a village, it was now a small town. The nearby research establishment had meant increased trade, had caused more houses to be built, had brought more traffic.

"That pub's prosperous," said Hill as they coasted along the main street. "More like a country club, I'd have said."

"Than what?" asked Green.

"Than a pub."

"Meaning they've put a couple of quids' worth of whitewash

9

on the walls, varnished the window frames and proceeded to charge twice as much for the beer?"

"I don't know, do I?"

The address of the research establishment may have suggested that it lay within the parish bounds of Pottersby. In reality, it was almost three and a half miles away from the village. Pottersby Hall, a sizeable house of probably thirty rooms, standing in its own grounds, had been taken over at the request of the last owner, who had sought by this means to lessen his *in vivo* expenses and his *post mortem* taxes. It probably made one of the poorest research bases—not being tailor-made for the job—but undoubtedly one of the prettiest. That is, if one ignored the double wire fences. These had been set up a dozen feet inside the perimeter wall which had, itself, been topped with barbed wire. Large notices proclaimed that guard dogs roamed at will in the space between the wall and the fences.

At they turned right off the road on the short indented approach to the main gate, Green said: "I've heard tell all boffins are crackers. And no wonder if they're cooped up behind wire like this. They might as well be in a loony bin or a nick."

The old main gate, wrought-iron and crested, still remained. So did the gatekeeper's cottage, though now this was used as a guardhouse.

"Detective Superintendent Masters' party," announced Brant to the uniformed gate policeman.

"All except you, get out and come in one at a time on foot." Masters didn't like it.

"I was told at Scotland Yard that I would be expected."

"A Superintendent Masters certainly is. If you're the genuine article, that's you. If not, you're in trouble, mate. Into the guardhouse."

The light was bright. They blinked against it as they showed their identification cards.

"One moment please." The guard in the office slid back a panel in the wall behind him. "Do you recognise Detective Inspector Green, sir?"

A voice from the room beyond said: "Of course I do. Willy P

in person!" The connecting door opened and a man of Green's age appeared.

"Remember me?"

"Widow!" said Green with surprise. "Widow Twankey!"

The two shook hands. "You moved out into Security, then?"

"Journeys may end in lovers' meetings," said Masters petulantly, "but I'm here, too, gooseberry-like."

"Toinquet, Chief Security Officer," said the newcomer. "Channel Island descent, third generation English."

"How do you do? It seems you have served with DI Green sometime in the past."

"When he was Sergeant Green. I've not seen him since 'fifty-five, but he hasn't changed much."

"Fine. Now how do I get to the Director?"

"I'll lead you up. My lads will have let your car through by now."

They rejoined Brant and followed Toinquet's VW along the drive. Modern road lights had been put up at close intervals along the way. After two hundred yards, as they neared the main house, it was possible to see that modern, single-storey structures had been erected on both sides of the old building.

They parked on the sweep of tarmac in front of the main door. By now it was almost dark. The Chief Security Officer led them in. The great hall of the house was uncarpeted. Notice-boards graced the walls and a barrack table served as a desk for the guard on duty.

"Director in his office, John?"

"I'll see, Mr Toinquet. These others had better sign in while I ring."

The visitors' book wanted to know it all. Name, status, department, nature of business, time in and—waiting for their return—time out.

"Doctor Crome's in. He'll see you now."

They all four toiled up to the first floor behind Toinquet. The government had seen fit to carpet the stairs with mole-coloured hair cord. It deadened the footsteps slightly.

The Director's office was the old master bedroom. Spacious,

and still decorated in white and gold, it was lit by a central chandelier, had an open fire blazing, and a circular dining table with half a dozen chairs in the middle of the floor as well as the Director's desk in the window.

"Doctor Crome: Detective Superintendent Masters."

To Masters' great surprise, Crome was not all that much older than himself. Forty or forty-two? A small man with a medium grey suit, well pressed, a neat shirt and tie and well-cleaned shoes. He had a mop of light brown, wavy hair, cut to give it shape and substance without running to sideboards or collar-length straggles.

They shook hands.

"You know my brief, sir," said Masters. "To establish whether your three scientists died from any cause other than accident, and if so, to solve any problem this poses."

"That's it. If you'd care to sit down—all of you—we can have a drink." He turned to Toinquet. "You, too, Michael. You're involved as much as any of us."

"I can't honestly see how, Doctor. I think the fact that the Yard has sent a murder team indicates they don't think that what has happened involves internal security. Otherwise the place would be thick with Special Branch."

Green, on hearing this, glanced at Masters. Masters, surprised by both the statement and the inimical content of Green's eye message, wondered how a chief security man could be so obtuse as to consider murder as unconnected with internal security and why Green was, apparently, not quite so friendly with his old colleague as Toinquet's initial welcome had suggested.

Crome was putting bottles of beer and glasses on the table. "Well at least stay and help me out if these four start shooting questions I can't answer."

The sat round the table.

"What do you want to know?" asked Crome.

"Everything you can safely tell us," replied Masters. "About this place, the three men who died, their jobs, hobbies, families, and anything else you can think of."

"Right. Chip in if you've got questions."

"No notes," said Toinquet.

Masters turned to him. "Throughout this investigation, I shall give the orders. Any reasonable request from you to me will, if I think it necessary, be translated into an order. I would like your co-operation on that basis, please."

Toinquet grunted—half agreement, half annoyance.

"Pottersby is not a major research centre," said Crome. "Not a Porton or a Harwell where there are major areas of study for specific purposes. We here are sweepers up. We have some relatively minor programmes under way—as a sort of skeleton of activity—but we spend much of our time on jobs which crop up. . . ."

"Unforeseen?"

"Very often. Let us say we supply answers to questions which crop up in the day-to-day running of a technocracy. Sometimes of a highly secret nature, sometimes not. Sometimes industrial, sometimes medical and sometimes military."

"Can you give us an example?"

"No, sir," said Toinquet. "Every job that comes here has a top classification, even if merely because the answer may lead to something of value."

"I see." Masters didn't suffer obstruction gladly, and privately he thought he and Toinquet were going to clash head-on before so very long.

"Perhaps," said Crome pacifically, "I could use a hypothetical case to which every platoon commander in the infantry could give you a reasoned answer. Let us say the Ministry of Defence was planning an invasion of Norway on a beach dominated by a hill five miles inland. They might like to use a nuclear weapon to destroy the enemy on the hill. Their likely questions would be something of this nature. We know we can use a tactical bomb so long as our own troops are not nearer to ground zero than three miles. But how soon can we put our own men on the hill to occupy it? Would it be safe to land troops from helicopters inside ten minutes? Or an hour? Or how long would we have to wait? How would the troops have to be equipped? How long could they stay?"

"You could provide the answers?"

"Maybe, maybe not. But we should try to do so. But as I said, the answers to that particular problem are already known, and I only used it to illustrate the fact that we here at Pottersby would not be asked to design a bomb, merely to answer some of the problems posed by its discovery and use."

"Thank you. I think I understand that point. Would you mind clarifying another? You say you have no formal long-term programme, yet I have been told that the three dead men, Doctors Redruth, Silk and Mailer—I take it he's dead by now—all came from the same team or department."

"Mailer is dead. I should have told you earlier. Yes, they are in a team, as every researcher is. Administratively it would be impossible for everybody to be a loner. My senior colleagues head-up firms or units. All the others belong to units which seem most appropriate to their general abilities. Any research worker who is needed elsewhere is temporarily loaned from his own unit to the one which needs his services. I find that it is necessary to do this actual physical shift, otherwise there could be a conflict of interests."

"Quite. So is it possible to know what the three we are interested in were engaged on?"

"Oddly enough, their unit is engaged on one of our few planned research projects. It is concerned with . . ."

"Steady, sir," warned Toinquet.

"Oh, yes! Security! Thank you, Michael. But I think I can give these four gentlemen just a general idea of what's going on in that area."

"As long as it is only general, Director."

"That particular unit—Group Six—is doing continuing tests on shielding for nuclear reactors. It's a long-term business."

"What does that mean?" asked Green. "Or can't we be told?"

"In layman's terms? Nuclear material is shielded by lead. As you know, you can power a ship by nuclear means if that ship is big enough to carry the weight. But quite powerful reactors can, themselves, be quite small, contained in, say, a twenty-inch cube. These could supply enough power to drive smaller ships or aircraft. But the weight of shielding necessary for safety would make them uneconomic. There'd be no payload. So Group Six is looking into reactor dynamics."

"With any hope of success?" asked Masters.

Crome smiled. "There's always hope. But I take your point. Shall we just say that should they be successful it would be a great breakthrough in many ways. Not only in providing a useful power source, but also in the disposal of atomic waste which, as you know, has to be shielded just as much as the active material."

"Thank you. We won't press for more details. But can I assume that the three dead men were all nuclear physicists?"

"You can."

"Top-flight men?"

Crome smiled again. "Mr Masters, all three were brilliant men —as I think you'd agree their qualifications would indicate. But what is regarded as a brilliant brain in the ordinary workaday world may only be regarded as average in a closed community such as this where so many are highly qualified. As I told you, we are not a major research station. So the really outstanding men—those recognised as such by their fellows—do not normally come here."

"I understand, Doctor. It explains why your Chief Security Officer regards the mysterious happenings here as a job for the CID rather than Special Branch."

"As Whitehall does," said Toinquet defensively.

"Quite. And believe me I mean no offence to your staff by suggesting they are so average as not to merit the attention of industrial or other espionage groups."

Crome said quietly: "We realise that, even though we take every possible precaution against such eventualities. But perhaps I have misled you. The three men who died were all young—in their early thirties. I think it safe to say that one—or even all three of them—would have graduated, with more experience, to the super league, although that is a description I deplore."

"Got it," said Green. "You use this place almost like a training course for bright youngsters as well as running it as a going concern in its own right."

"I couldn't have put it better myself, Mr Green."

Green looked pleased with himself and slurped the remains of his beer.

"Now," said Masters, "what about mountaineering?"

Toinquet took up the running.

"It's one of those things with leading scientists. By and large they're loners. They won't indulge in team games. Yet they like the exercise. Wherever I've been as a Security Officer there's been a mountaineering and walking club."

"Club?" asked Green with mock surprise. "Same as team, isn't it, Widow?"

"Hardly. The club part of it is only for administration. The exercise part is every man for himself."

Brant leaned forward. "Does that mean that when they aren't mountaineering or get too old for it they have no interests other than their work?"

"Of course not. A surprising number of them make music."

"Compose?"

"No. They play. Often quite badly. But two or three of them will get together and immerse themselves in making music. That's what they call it themselves. On occasions it's the most excruciating row imaginable, but they do it and enjoy it."

"Don't forget our dramatic society," said Crome. "Very thriving. We have quite a few women here, you know—employees as well as wives."

"They're interested in play acting?"

"Of course. It follows the pattern Michael has been outlining. An actor must be an egoist. Anyhow, when they appear they are pandering to their sense of self-importance or self-centredness in character. Nobody else is involved when they're doing their bit of showing off."

"This is very interesting," said Masters. "I've been wondering why two of the men who were killed were climbing solo when I had always believed mountaineers went roped."

"You're talking about normal clubs," said Toinquet. "Where there are rules and regulations. Our people here consider such precautions an affront or a deprivation of liberty or some such

16

tarradiddle. Comes of living behind barbed wire all the time, I expect."

"There's something in what Michael says," added Crome. "Just as people who live in these high-rise flats get neuroses, so do our people here. You know, it is terribly difficult for them. They are supposed to take mental leaps in the dark—to tread where nobody else has ever trodden before—and yet they are confined physically within a guarded perimeter. And even when they're outside it they cannot discuss their work. The trouble that constraint causes—particularly to the less conservative among us—is immense."

"I can imagine it."

"Some of them are arrogant," asserted Toinquet. "They think they can do what others can't—that they're indestructible on mountains, in snowstorms, rain and mist. It's really an unbelievable trait in highly intelligent men."

"So with the three you've lost," said Green, "it could literally have been a case of pride coming before the fall?"

"That would be too easy a conclusion," said Crome. "They were all able climbers, weren't they, Michael?"

"Oddly enough, Director, those three were. In fact, from my observations, I'd have said they were three of the few who really had their heads screwed on properly round here."

Masters said nothing, but drummed with one finger on the table. Crome got up to open more bottles of beer. As he placed one beside Masters he said: "You're looking a bit pensive, Super. Is something we've said troubling you?"

"I think so. Able climbers falling from easy slopes sounds bad. When the climbers are all brilliant young men destined for higher things it sounds even worse."

"You mean it makes murder look more likely?"

"Doesn't it to you?"

"I have never doubted it was murder—after Mailer's fall, that is."

"Ah! Then you must have some fact on which to base your opinion. As a scientist you would not accept an unsubstantiated belief as being beyond doubt."

Crome sat down. "You're not slow at catching on."

"Please don't insult me. This isn't the first case I've investigated."

"I apologise. Even I know something of your reputation, and I'd have said I was as unworldly as any man—being one of the lunatic boffins shut up in his own little scientific sphere."

"Not so," replied Masters. "To be the Director of a government research centre means you have to be extremely aware of what goes on—politically, at any rate. You need to deal with Whitehall more than most. But that is by the way. Your reason for being confident it was murder, Doctor Crome, if you please."

"Egg-heads like us tend to belong to chosen schools of thought. I'll explain that. Take astronomers as an example. The two main schools on the formation of the universe are the big-bang merchants and the steady-state adherents. So in other forms of physics. Over certain premises we tend to polarise. Nobody disagrees on pure basics, but they do on directions and uses if not on more abstruse questions."

"How abstruse?"

"Well, I don't want to talk above your heads—which is a common failing among people like us—but there is the argument raging here about whether parity is conserved or not."

"You are above my head already."

Crome laughed. "In layman's terms again, it's the argument as to whether the physical universe is more left-handed than right-handed or vice versa, or whether it is absolutely impartial."

Green grunted in disbelief. "You mean that is a bone of contention among your people?"

"I'm not talking about human beings, but about particle physics," explained Crome. "One school says parity is preserved, others say it is not. The older men tend to belong to the former school, the younger ones to the latter. These young people assert it has been proved that with certain particles, at least, there is no mirror image of reactions and interactions—almost like Newton's old law of equal and opposite reactions which you will have heard of. Our three dead men were all members of the school who believe that parity is not conserved. Now I'm not saying that this particular argument has any bearing on the tragedies. I'm just using it as an illustration of the fact that there are deep professional divisions among us."

"But you are, nevertheless, suggesting that professional disagreement among your scientists could have led to these three deaths."

"I have made the point advisedly—in the interests of your investigation." He spread his hands. "I was bound to think something of the sort, particularly as most of the others here believe that parity in nature *is* conserved. These three men were linked so indissolubly in the way they met their deaths, their ages, their abilities, their schools of thought, their work, their department . . . need I go on?"

"No, Doctor. But I can't believe they were killed because they believe nature is not impartial."

"Your decisions or beliefs are for you to arrive at. You have come in from outside. It should be easier for you to make a reasonable assessment than it is for me working here among these people."

Masters took out his pipe. "We've talked about mountaineering. Did Mr Toinquet say there was a walking club as well?"

"It's the same club," said the Security man. "What usually happens is that climbers and walkers go off together at week-ends in the same coach. It's the cheapest way. They go to Wales, the Lake District and—particularly when there's a long break as at Easter and Whit—to Scotland or wherever so that those who want to climb can do so, and the rest can walk."

"Not private cars?"

"It's unusual for them to take cars. They're not highly paid, you know. The pennies count. A hired coach comes cheaper. Particularly as they have one most week-ends in the year."

"Always the same blokes?" asked Green.

"Not by a long chalk. I think there are nearly a couple of hundred in the club. Some are keener than others, of course."

"Women, too?"

Toinquet nodded. "Quite a number of tough young birds here, though they're usually in the walking parties."

"Anybody keep lists of who goes on these trips?"

"I do. I keep a note of everything. You should know that."

"Then you know what I was going to ask."

"I do. How many people were present on all three occasions when the deaths occurred."

"Well?"

"No mountaineers. Some walkers. But I might as well tell you that when each of those three fell, they were seen to be alone on their climbs, and the walkers were all some distance away."

"They were seen to be climbing alone and to fall?"

"Yes."

"Who by?"

"Other climbers and various people who go along to fill up the bus. They don't climb or walk. They picnic or camp or just watch or take films. There's usually a party of two or three of them. Wives sometimes."

Crome looked at his watch. "Anything more for the moment? I shall be available whenever you wish to see me, of course, but I have an engagement in a few minutes' time."

"There are quite a lot more questions to be answered," admitted Masters, who felt less than pleased that an important murder investigation should be interrupted virtually at the outset for what he could only assume—as it was Sunday evening—would be a social occasion. Probably a cocktail party, judging by the early hour.

"In that case, perhaps I could seek you out later. Meantime, I will hand you over to Michael who will see you into your quarters and show you the mess dining room and bar."

Green pushed his chair back. "You're putting us up while we're here?"

"I assumed that is what you'd like me to do. We've got the room. There's the pub in the village, of course, but I doubt whether you'd get four beds at such short notice."

"We shall do very well here," said Masters. "Thank you, Doctor, for the offer."

"Right then," said Toinquet. "This way, gentlemen."

Chapter 2

To the surprise of Masters who, for no very sound reason, had thought the living quarters would be in the main house, they were ushered out of a side door and along a narrow concrete path towards one of the modern blocks.

"Does nobody live in the house?" he asked as they went.

"Only the Director. He has a large flat up there. The rest of it is given over to admin offices, central registry, library and so on. My private office is in there, too."

"It seems to me like the waste of a gracious home."

Toinquet didn't reply. Masters didn't know whether the Security Officer agreed or disagreed on this point, but darkness and the narrowness of the way did not make for easy conversation, and the party fell silent as they went along in single file.

"It's all here," said Toinquet as they stepped inside the double swing doors of the single-storey complex and stopped in front of a glass-fronted notice-board. "The complete lay-out of the living quarters if you're interested."

The diagram showed the building to be in the shape of a capital H. The main entrance—the one they had just used—was at the western end of the crosspiece. The north and south running arms of the first upright were devoted entirely to study-bedrooms, with bathrooms at either end. The southern half of the second upright was given over to similar rooms. The northern half of the second upright was, however, differently divided. In the centre of it, directly opposite the main doorway where they were now congregated, was a games and TV room, then an office—presumably the mess office. Next door to this, a bar. After that, the corridor was included in a very large room—the ante room—which in turn led to one of similar size—the dining room. Beyond this—where the bathrooms were in the other wings—were kitchens and boiler room.

The corridors were on the inside of each wing, with rooms on the outside only. The area enclosed on the north by the arms of the H was labelled Car Park, that to the south Lawn and Drying Ground.

"Drying Ground?" queried Green.

"Linen lines," replied Toinquet. "Lots of people wash their own smalls at week-ends. They hang them out there. Why, lord only knows. There's a perfectly good airing room for that sort of thing, but this lot will tell you that things smell sweeter dried in the open. Sweeter! I ask you! The place looks like a back street in Naples in decent weather, just when people want to put a deckchair out there."

"Seems reasonable to me," answered Green. From the way in which the DI made this remark, Masters guessed he was trying to be perverse, and his next words proved it. "If cleanliness is next to Godliness, Widow, and you're nearer God's heart in a garden, you've got the best of both worlds. Or are you frightened the girls are giving ground-to-air signals of a secret nature every time they hang their knickers on the line?"

Toinquet didn't rise to that one, but went on to point out to Masters that there were subsidiary doors in the middle of each of the near wings and the central corridor which gave on to the car park and the lawns.

"So," he continued, "all your rooms are down this corridor on the left. Bathrooms and lavatories at the end. Be careful with the loos. One's reserved for women."

The floors were covered in heavy brown vinyl, the unplastered walls cream-washed, the paintwork a gloss brown that reminded Masters of the hard brightness of pottery horses. The place was spotless.

"Numbers six and seven, eleven and twelve. All ready made up. Keys in the doors. I'll see you in."

"Can I bring the car round?" asked Brant.

"Sorry. Yes. This park here is reserved for living-in members' cars." Toinquet stopped at one of the corridor windows. The asphalt patch already held several vehicles. "Bring it in there and park it just close to this side door down here."

As Toinquet saw Masters into his room, he said: "Cold supper on a Sunday. You help yourself from the side table between seven-thirty and eight-fifteen. Sign the book inside the door as having eaten."

"That gives us a few minutes for a wash."

"Bags of time. You've got a washbasin in here as you can see. There's a staff for making beds and so on, all as trustworthy as can be, but if you've got anything confidential, let me know and I'll allot you a secure cupboard in depository."

"Thanks. There is one more thing, Mr Toinquet." The Security Officer stood silent, waiting. "When I investigate a case, I do so without fear or favour. I also expect co-operation and complete candour, particularly from somebody like yourself who should—everything else being equal—be on our side."

"I don't see your point—unless you think I'm hiding something."

"Are you?"

"I'm a Chief Security Officer. I've more secrets in my head than anybody else round here."

"I appreciate that. Are there any of those secrets you should be sharing with me?"

"Of course not. You may be a top policeman, but this is official secrets stuff. Nobody gets it out of me."

Masters considered the man for a moment. Took in his window-pane check suit with its hacking jacket long-skirted and full—too full—the club tie, the high-gloss shoes, and decided, bearing in mind that it was late Sunday afternoon and therefore time for dressing down, not up, that here was a vain man. Was it his vanity that caused him to be so prickly, or something more?

"Hey, Widow!" Green stuck his head round the door. "Sergeant Brant can't get in with the bags."

The confrontation was at an end.

"Sorry. I'll unlock." Toinquet turned back to Masters. "OK, Super, I'll be in the ante room if you'll join me there when you're ready." The invitation sounded to Masters more like a challenge than a friendly gesture.

"Like some of the better army billets," said Green a quarter of an hour later as all four of them made their way together to the mess area. "I suppose they have to shove these places up in the Centres that are miles from anywhere—for the unmarrieds and visitors and such like."

The ante room was furnished from government stock. A huge red carpet with grey medallions four feet across that gave it a dusty air; chairs, all of a kind, upholstered in red and brown washable vinyl; round teak coffee tables. But the room had the comfort of an open fire. It was deserted except for Toinquet who stood, one hand on the brick mantelpiece, one foot on the scuffed curb.

"We can have a drink in here if you want to sit, or we can go to the bar next door and stand."

"Bar, sir, please," pleaded Hill. "We've been sitting all afternoon and I must say a drink always tastes better in a bar."

The bar was a small room, no more than fifteen feet square, leading off the ante room. The walls had been decorated, cartoon-like, with more amateur enthusiasm than professional skill. The bar counter took up two-thirds of one side. Behind it was a barman in a white jacket talking to his solitary customer. As the five entered, Toinquet addressed the latter's back. "Good evening, Doctor."

The man turned and stared in surprise.

"Good heavens! Masters, isn't it? And full crew? You remember me? Partington?"

Masters grinned. "Good evening, Dr Partington. Yes, we're all here." They shook hands. "Three years ago, wasn't it? The case in Oldham where the young woman died as a result of criminal assault?"

"That's it. I had to help with the gory details."

"Yes. Nasty business, that."

"You all know each other?" asked Toinquet in some surprise. Masters got the impression that Toinquet was perturbed by the

24

knowledge. But the Security Officer's recuperative powers were working well. His next words sounded normal enough.

"Fine. Now, what'll who have?"

The party broke up into small groups.

"You've come to solve the mystery of our three dead boffins, I suppose," said Partington.

"That's it," replied Masters. "I must say it's pleasant to find a face one knows in a place like this. But tell me, how does a provincial GP find himself in a research centre?"

"I'm the resident quack."

"Purely medical?"

"If you mean simply to look after the health of the hired help and their families, not quite. I do that, of course, but I'm also involved in any facet of the research that impinges on matters medical."

"I see. How come?"

"As a matter of fact, that case in Oldham really started me off. Caroline Benson . . ."

"The girl who died?"

Partington nodded. "She wasn't a girl really, you know. She was a very attractive young woman of four-and-twenty."

Masters looked at him closely.

"Yes," said Partington. "If she hadn't been one of my patients . . . well, that made me slow off the mark. It was my first practice job, and I was very conscious of the doctor/patient relationship. Otherwise, I think we'd have got together . . ."

"I didn't know," said Masters gently. "Believe me, I'm very sorry."

"There was nothing settled. Only hope on my side. But her death decided me. I'd always been keen on the physics side, so I applied for a two-year post-graduate course in nuclear medicine."

"With this sort of thing in mind?"

"Not really. I was toying with the thought of Canada. They have a lakeside place out there—White Plains, I think it's called —where they are concentrating on the medical side. Plenty of openings there for the properly qualified, with first-class working conditions and good pay."

"What stopped you?"

"Heaven knows! Would you believe patriotism or something akin?"

"I would. I'm very aware of it within myself."

"I suppose you are. A chap of your calibre would be welcome anywhere. I'm surprised the FBI hasn't lured you away. Anyway, when I got to the end of my course I decided that if I was going to apply for jobs I'd better have a reference from the head of the faculty. When I approached him he said the British government had a job for me if I would consider taking it. I agreed. After all, he'd accepted me for the course and they'd paid for my training. So I found myself here about fourteen months ago."

"Can I get you another drink?" asked Masters.

"Not before we eat if you don't mind. We can wander through now if you like."

As they moved, Masters asked Partington if he was still unmarried.

"I'm to be a June groom," he said with a grin. "The junior partner in the Pottersby Health Centre is a bonny, bouncing, well-covered Scots lassie with a degree in medicine and a belief in the National Health Service."

"And in you, too, by the sound of it."

"She keeps that aspect well hidden. Ah! Here we are. Cold cuts. That looks like rabbit. Cold beef pie—usually very good. No bully, I'm afraid...and yes, cold mutton. Help yourself. Spud salad, beetroot, pickles..."

They loaded their plates and took places at one of the tables. By now several newcomers who had not been in the bar were entering the dining room.

"I see the party has got back from Wales."

Masters looked about him. A middle-aged man in knee breeches, stockings, fell boots and roll-neck sweater was helping himself to food. A few feet away from him, a woman, square-built, in a tweed skirt and bottle-green corduroy lumber jacket, brown walking shoes and rolled-down socks, was shaking salad cream from a bottle.

"Those two?"

26

Partington nodded. "Cecil Winter and Dorothy Clay. Both walkers. Winter is secretary of the club."

The two selected a table some distance away. It was clear they were fond of the outdoors. Winter was scrawny, hawk-like, with a bald patch as brown and weather-beaten as his face. Dorothy Clay, Masters estimated, would be about forty. She, too, was weather-beaten, but not unattractively so. She had a round face with a button of a nose, short-length hair and a strong, comfortable figure, not very tall, but compact.

"Are they both living-in members?"

"Oh, yes. Clay, I'm afraid, is a reluctant spinster . . ."

"Meaning she's reluctant to remain one or reluctant to relinquish her single status?"

"The former. She's feller-fond, as they say in Oldham. But in liking them she adopts so many of their mannerisms that she lessens her chances more than she increases them."

"Definitely one of the boys, is she?"

"She likes her pint and her hill-walking."

"Winter?"

"He's a married man, but his wife stays on at her own home. As I understand it she was reluctant to give it up for a two- or three-year tour here in rented accommodation. And I don't blame her. From what I hear, they own a delectable dwelling made from knocking two picturesque cottages into one and installing all mod cons."

"Odd, that."

"How so?"

"He climbs or walks at week-ends in preference to going home. Or is it so far away he can't get home easily?"

"Down in Dorset. Not all that far."

"And what does he do here?"

"He's the leader of Group Six."

"The group the three dead men were in?"

"Yes. But damp down your interest a bit. He's not a bad old stick, and he never climbs."

Masters made a mental note to ask Toinquet whether Winter was one of those walkers who had been members of all the parties on which the fatalities had occurred. Not that walkers who were miles away from the scene of the fall in each case could conceivably be implicated. But all the ground had to be covered.

"I haven't yet seen the post-mortem reports on Redruth and Silk," said Masters. "Have you got copies of the medical evidence in your files by any chance?"

"Lord, no. There was no reason for them to be sent here. They were kept, as usual, in the localities where the accidents happened and where the inquests were held."

"I wonder whether you could save me the bother of asking for them to be sent down here. I shall get the one on Mailer from the police in North Wales as a matter of course now that foul play is suspected."

"Anything I can do to help, I will."

Masters pushed his plate to one side. "There is something I would particularly like. The first two, Redruth and Silk, died when they hit the ground. Obviously the post-mortems showed nothing untoward, otherwise there'd have been inquiries made at the time. So I'm going to learn nothing from them."

"Nor from this last one, I suspect."

"But there's a difference this time. Mailer lived for some hours. A doctor must have reached him fairly soon. I want a report from that doctor."

"He'll speak at the inquest. Get a transcript."

"I don't want an official report. I prefer something on the old-boy net. Ask the medic what he thought had happened, not what he reported."

"You're not going to get anything. Mailer may have still been alive, but he was concussed. There wouldn't have been any verbal clues given, and broken bodies tell you little when they've fallen several hundred feet on to a jumble of rocks—to say nothing of hitting a few on the way down. After a post-mortem you may get a few more facts, but only as to which bones were fractured and which not."

Masters tapped the table. "Look, I'm up against it here. I know the business stinks of murder, but even at this early stage I know I'm on a sticky wicket. So I've got to explore not only reasonable possibilities, but unreasonable ones, too. And I want a spontaneous report from that doctor. Not an official one. That's why I don't want to ask the North Wales police to approach him."

"In that case, get me his name and address and I'll phone him. But he may not be willing to play."

Partington was showing all the reluctance of the medical profession to interfere in matters which are not strictly their business —despite his words. Masters couldn't see the objection. To him, the gathering of information was more important than professional reticence.

"You were Mailer's GP, weren't you? You're entitled to know all the little ethical secrets."

"And pass them on to you? I like that!"

"Can I get you some more coffee?" asked Masters blithely.

Green was eating with Toinquet.

"Come on, Widow, out with it." Green sawed a forkful from a slice of mutton.

"Out with what?"

"Your off-the-record idea about these deaths. And don't tell me you haven't got one. No Security man of your experience would let three of his little lambs die without having some thoughts as to how they came to get the chop."

"No ideas at all, Greeny."

"You're a liar," said Green complacently. "You'll be telling me next that the thought had never occurred to you that those boyos hadn't slipped, but were pushed."

"I don't see why both you and Masters think I'm hiding something."

"So he thinks so, too, does he? Why didn't you tell Crome that he should ask for an investigation?" The content of the question was pure guesswork on Green's part, but it seemed to be right on target. "You must have had some reason."

"I was going to, but I was beaten to it by Whitehall."

"In that case, you must have had a good reason for intending to."

"Coincidences," said Toinquet, sounding a little short on temper.

"When things happen in threes—being paid to be a suspicious man—I naturally get suspicious."

"Pull the other one. If three of these blokes won a couple of hundred each on the pools in the same period it would be just as big a coincidence, but I'll bet you wouldn't turn a hair. But you're turning hairs now. Your wig's so bloody crimped you could use it for a switchback at Battersea fun fair."

"You're getting clever in your old age, Greeny. So I'll tell you. I'm into everything here, including the mountaineering and walking club. It's obvious why. They push off alone, outside my bailiwick. It's an opportunity some fly boy might seize to do something stupid."

"Like passing over a few secrets?"

"I know it sounds daft, but it has been done; and that's what I'm here to prevent."

"Any thoughts on which of them might try anything like that?"

"No. If I had, I'd watch them closer than a dog watching a bone."

"No coincidences about these week-end trips to make you suspicious?"

"Only these deaths."

"Do you mean that there are no coincidences, or just that there are no suspicious coincidences?"

Toinquet waved his knife in the air. "Well of course there'll be coincidences if I looked for them. If I analysed everybody's movements . . ."

"Hold it," growled Green. "If you don't look for them, how the hell do you know there are no suspicious coincidences?"

"I meant none that spring to the eye in the normal course of events."

"That doesn't square up with what you've just said about being into everything here in case some fly boy pulls a fast one."

"How d'you mean?"

"You suggested that you look closely at every activity, then you said you meant that the only coincidences you are likely to spot are those that spring readily to the eye. Which is it?"

Toinquet put down his knife and fork. "Now look here,

Greeny, you're beginning to get up my nose." He leaned forward, speaking quietly but venomously. "You come here and start throwing your weight around. . . ."

"Who, me?" asked Green in mock surprise. "Come off it, Widow. You know the score—or you damn well should do. There's nothing personal in this. If there was, I'd be asking you why you weren't suspicious of the second climbing death. The first one, even. But I'm not. I've never mentioned them."

"You're hinting I've fallen down on my job."

"Only because I've got a great respect for your ability, Widow."

"What does that mean?" The Security Officer sounded slightly mollified, but still wary.

Green pulled a dish of rhubarb towards him and took up his spoon. "Well, old mate, if you say you're into everything here, then I'm pretty sure it will be all buttoned up and there'll be no hanky-panky going unspotted, because you know your game. But —and this is where there's a big discrepancy . . ." He took a spoonful of rhubarb. "I say, Widow, this is good. When I was a lad I used to train for the school sports on rhubarb. Blood-shot celery we used to call it. . . ."

"What's this big discrepancy you were rabbiting on about?"

"Why, the fact that there *was* some obvious hanky-panky going on despite the fact that you were keeping an eye on things."

"You haven't proved there was."

"True. But you said yourself you were so sure there was that you were going to urge the Director to call in the Yard if Whitehall hadn't beaten you to it."

"I said that was because of the coincidence."

"That's right. You did. But you're not going to tell me that a chap of your calibre has to wait for a coincidence to hit him in the eye before he takes action."

"This was three deaths. Of course it hit me in the eye."

"Meaning you didn't ask yourself a few questions after the second death? Two deaths in precisely similar circumstances constitute a coincidence too, you know."

31

"What questions could I ask? I wasn't there when the fatalities occurred."

"Neither were we, but we're asking questions."

"Meaning I should have carried out an investigation after Redruth fell?"

"Why not?"

"How far would I have got?"

"I don't know. But even if you weren't successful, you might have saved Mailer."

"How d'you make that out?"

"The mere fact that you were going round asking questions might have put somebody off trying again. That might have saved Mailer and saved us from having to poke our noses in, which you don't seem to like over much, Widow."

"I don't."

"I wonder why?"

"This is my patch. . . ."

"Borax!" Green scraped his dish clean and smacked his lips over the last of the rhubarb. "If it's your patch, Widow, you want to keep it free of weeds. And anybody who wants to do that welcomes a friendly hand to help him. Let's face it, you don't call in an expert gardener and then try to stop him working just because it's your bit of land."

"Have it your way, Greeny."

"Not my way, boyo. Masters' way. And he's a bastard. It's no secret him and me don't hit it off. I can just hear what he's going to say about you in that supercilious voice of his."

"Oh, yes! What?"

"Well, you've got to appreciate that Masters thinks he's the ultimate, and that nobody, but nobody, could object to his presence—unless they had something personal to hide. That being so, the first thing he's going to say about you—and he'll have his nose in the air when he says it—is that he reckons you'll bear watching. And when he says watching, he means hounding to death."

"Let him," said Toinquet.

"If that's all you've got to say," murmured Green, selecting a crumpled Kensitas, "where's all this chit-chat getting us?"

"Getting us? Getting you, you mean. All I've been trying to point out is that I've been on some of these week-end trips. I saw all those three chaps climb, and believe me, they could climb. And that's not only my opinion, either. So why did they all fall from easy pitches? That's what you and Masters should be asking, not hounding me. Christ, man, I'm wanting results as much as you are, even if I don't want you here."

"Why were two of them climbing alone?"

"Because they were on such easy pitches. That's my point. We're always talking about people not acting out of character and leopards not changing their spots. If you accept that, then you have to accept that good climbers don't crash from easy pitches. Not three of them, at any rate."

"I'd still like to know why two of them were climbing alone. I'll even accept your explanation for the first chap. But after a fatality, surely the climbing discipline is tightened up?"

Toinquet sounded exasperated. "We've been through all that. The important thing in climbing is the personal element."

"But that doesn't mean climbing alone," said Green stubbornly. "All it means is that it's up to you and your pals on the same rope to make your own decisions as the need crops up. It doesn't mean being so free—or so high an' mighty—that you do your own thing on your own."

Toinquet sighed. "You don't know this crowd. They're not like ordinary people. Honest, they're not. They're nice men and women, but they're crackers."

"Intense?"

"That's the word. Inner driving force like a coiled-up spring. I tell you, Greeny, that this lot would go off on a difficult climb alone just out of pure pig-iron if you were to remind them of the dangers."

"Yeah?"

"They'd smile and say that the higher the penalty for failure is likely to be, the greater the reward for success. And that, they will argue, is the most personally satisfying of the attractions of climbing."

"Something I *would* like to ask you about," said Masters as he and Partington carried their coffee cups into the ante room, "is Crome's standing in the hierarchy of boffins."

"I don't think I understand you. Or if I do, I don't know whether I'm sufficiently aware of the comparative abilities of senior scientists or the regard in which they are held by their peers."

They selected two chairs set well away from the others in the big room.

"I want to talk generalisations," said Masters. "And for that reason, I ask you, as an outsider, to give me your opinion. I don't feel I can ask one of Crome's own scientists—for obvious reasons—and even if I were to do so, I'd probably be blinded with parochial details I don't want."

"In that case, fire away. But remember Crome is my boss, too, and I'm not entirely devoid of a feeling of loyalty simply because my discipline differs from his."

"He gave me to understand that Pottersby is very much in the second division of research centres; that it doesn't compare either in facilities or standard of staff with Harwell or Porton, for instance. Is that mock modesty or fact?"

Partington shrugged his shoulders. "He's right, to some degree. We tend to be a jack-of-all-trades centre. But only in so far as the work is more diverse, not less technical. Nor are the problems posed and resolved here less puzzling than elsewhere."

"And Crome himself?" Masters felt he could safely introduce the name now Partington was talking freely. "Is he less than outstanding that he should become head of a lesser institution?"

This time Partington chuckled aloud. "If he gave you that impression, he was pulling your leg unmercifully."

"Why should he do that?"

"Even among top-flight boffins, and people who select and appoint them, there are human weaknesses which a realistic chap like yourself would find unbelievable."

34

"Try me."

"Directors of places such as this obviously have to be able scientists, but in addition they have to be skilled administrators and diplomats of a high order."

"In order to allocate work and keep a lot of highly temperamental staff sweet and friendly?"

"That's it. And so, in choosing a man to head up a place like Pottersby, there has to be a lot of careful selection done."

"And lobbying? And personal animosities catered for? And compromise? And all the rest of the ballyhoo?"

"You've got the picture. Now take ability as a scientist, which is obviously the first prerequisite for such a post. How would you decide which of a dozen worthy men, all with much the same experience and the same numbers of letters after their names, should be chosen as the Director of Pottersby?"

"I'm doubtful whether anybody could make such a choice without knowing all the candidates personally—knowing them well enough, that is, to be aware of their strengths and weaknesses. And among those latter, these days, I suppose one must consider political affiliations or bias, potential for becoming a blackmail victim, and all the other unsavoury facets of character."

"You've obviously had some experience on selection boards involving appointments where security is a factor."

"I haven't. I'm trying to be the realist you very kindly said I was."

"Fair enough. But having satisfactorily eliminated the perverts, the incurable alcoholics and debtors, the fanatical and so on, what then?"

"You tell me."

"This is where the human frailty comes in. There are usually some selectors who have favourites among the candidates. Those who are uncommitted, however, seek for a sign for guidance."

"In what guise?"

"Usually in publications. A leading man who has read papers hither, thither and yon, and has appeared in print in the scientific journals, begins to get known as a leading light. So he has a head start."

"But?"

"This sort of caper is all very fine for the man who is involved in work which is important but which is not cloaked in the secrecy demanded by Security. He can write and talk as much as he likes, doing his own PR job. But the chap who beavers away successfully on some work which is so hush-hush that even the Research Council members themselves aren't aware of it, has no big drum to beat. Continuing the orchestral analogy, there is nobody to blow his trumpet in the councils of the mighty except, possibly, his own boss, should he be consulted."

"And the boss, presumably, would not wish to lose so useful a colleague."

"Quite. There ain't no fairness. It often takes a long time for silent ability to be fully recognised, and when it is, it is not accepted without trial, as it were."

"I get it. Crome was a non-publisher."

"He was almost forbidden to breathe. But the sheer brilliance of the man eventually broke through the clouds obscuring him. So he was sent here. He knows he's being given an audition for a bigger role."

"For a Directorship at one of the major centres?"

"One supposes so. But he would likely go as a Deputy Director in the first place. And that's a pity, because though he's a good administrator and diplomat, a Deputy Director is more of a quartermaster, if such illustrious men will forgive the analogy. I mean they are more responsible for providing the buildings and buying the test tubes than for directing the research itself."

"But even to do that one would need to know what one was about—scientifically, I mean."

"Naturally. But it is a housekeeping role, nonetheless."

Masters put his coffee cup down.

"Thank you for being so frank. I'm beginning to get the background now. But just one more question. If Crome is on trial here, will the business I'm investigating affect him adversely?"

"My guess is that it all depends on how you manage to play it. But it can't do him any positive good. Scandals and publicity about a place like this are frowned on officially, and the Director is very responsible."

"Very responsible?"

"He is curbed and watched pretty closely in the interests of finance, security and so on. But the place, the people and the work are all his."

"And the results?"

"Lord knows who they belong to! In name, they belong to the great British public who fund the work. But they're rarely allowed to know the extent of their corporate possessions."

Masters got to his feet. "I've been neglecting my flock."

"I'll bet. If I know you, you gave them instructions to make individual contacts among the few of us in mess and to pump for all they're worth."

Masters grinned. "I assure you I gave no such instruction."

"So they didn't need it. It's a standing order. I noticed Green had buttonholed Toinquet before supper."

"They're old buddies. Joined the force together years ago, but Toinquet moved to a security section and has stayed with the work ever since. He preferred it to being a policeman."

"And your sergeants? They weren't in the dining room."

"That's what I just said. I've been neglecting them."

"Right. I'll leave you to your Bo-Peep act. I'll not forget the doctor's original observations on Mailer—if he made any."

"If he didn't, he's a foolish man, with the likelihood of an inquest staring him in the face."

"You've no idea just how foolish an overworked GP can sometimes be."

It was just after Masters and Partington had left the bar to have supper that Hill, stepping backwards to allow one of the newly returned climbers and walkers to get up to the counter, jogged the arm of another drinker.

"Sorry, sir."

The man wiped a few drops of beer from his jacket. "No harm done. It's man-made fibre. A drop of ale won't stain it, but it'll make it smell good."

"Can I get you another to top up, sir?"

"I didn't lose more than ten mils. And what's all this sir stuff?"

"Policemen are supposed to be polite to members of the public," said Hill.

"Copper, are you?"

"Detective Sergeant Hill."

"I'm Alec Bullock."

"Scientist, sir?"

"Sort of. Tame mathematician, actually, though I'm listed as Chief Statistician."

Hill guessed Bullock to be about forty. He had all the appearance of a middle-aged, switched-on trendy. The fair hair, though sparse, was long enough to hang over the collar of the grey-green anorak. The floral shirt peeped less than coyly from behind the zipped front; the necktie, held together in front by a brass ring, shouted at it; and the fingers that held the beer were beringed and none too clean in appearance.

"Four of us are down here to look into the death of Dr Mailer."

"So I heard. Pity about Clive buying it! Not a bad chap!"

"You knew him well, sir?"

Bullock said: "Cut out this sir lark, Sergeant. Call me Alec, Alexander, Sandy, or simply Bullock, but don't call me sir."

"Right. Did you know Dr Mailer well?"

"What is this? An inquisition?"

"If you like. Three scientists have been killed while climbing. Hundreds of miles apart. We can't hope to get to know why unless we ask questions. So we're asking questions—of everybody."

Bullock considered Hill for a moment, measuring him, the sergeant supposed, like an equation put down for the solving.

"OK. I knew Clive pretty well. I did his sums for him when he wanted me to and we drank together occasionally in the village."

"Not in here?"

"He was a married man. Lived out."

"But at lunchtimes?"

"Clive drank very little."

"But you said you met him in the pub occasionally."

"So I did. He wasn't a teetotaller, and his missus liked a drink in company. A lot of us use the pub. It's one of our few recreational facilities within striking distance. The drinks are dearer than in here, but we can't live cooped up the whole time."

Hill got the impression that Bullock wanted to leave it at that. His glass was empty and he seemed set to leave. But the sergeant was too much of a professional to break off a conversation which might still yield information.

"Dr Mailer liked mountaineering? Was that to keep physically fit? Or didn't he drink much in order to keep fit for climbing?"

Bullock held out his hand for Hill's glass. "Come on, have the other half."

"I'm doing nicely, thank you."

"A short then. I'm going to have one."

"Not for me. This isn't my first, you know."

"I'll get you one. A double. Bell's."

Hill felt it unwise to argue further. He edged away to a less crowded part of the little room to wait for Bullock. The mathematician's attitude intrigued him. Bullock gave the impression of not wanting to talk, but against all reason was proposing to do so—fortified by drink to make the undertaking easier. Hill felt a tingle of pleasure: the compulsive talker who really has something to contribute and is not simply a gasbag is a godsend to a policeman.

"Here you are. I put in water—fifty, fifty."

Hill thanked him.

"You asked me if Clive Mailer liked mountaineering," reminded Bullock.

"And you didn't answer."

"How the hell could I? A soft bloody word such as 'liked'! He was a mountaineer. A good one. And an enthusiast."

Bullock downed his own Scotch in a single gulp and, without another word, turned again towards the bar. When he came back he said, "I'm going to get as tight as a tick, Sergeant."

"Just like that?" The feeling Hill had about this man was

reinforced. A reason for insobriety in the face of a police investigation could mean anything. But it had to mean something. Guilt? Guilty knowledge?

"Why not?"

"You must have some good reason. What I mean is . . ."

"I know fine what you mean. You can understand somebody getting tanked up, inadvertently as it were, as an evening progresses. But you can't see the sense in announcing that you're going to drink yourself into oblivion."

"That's right. I can't."

"Why don't you add 'when a Scotland Yard man is asking questions?' It's a new experience for you, is it? Well, let me tell you, Sergeant—and you needn't stare at me to see if I'm still sober, I am—that I feel like the biggest lump of excreta there's ever been. And shall I tell you why?"

"I'd like to hear."

Bullock drained his glass. Hill wondered whether to try and stop the statistician having another so that he would remain lucid now that he was about to talk, or whether to lubricate him a little more to further loosen his tongue. Bullock solved the problem. He held out his glass. "Your round, I believe. Let's have one on police expenses." The words were just beginning to slur.

With his third quick double in his hand and the first two already augmenting the effect of the beer he had drunk initially, Bullock showed every sign of growing confidential.

"You were saying you were feeling at cross purposes with yourself," prompted Hill.

"Thass a nice way of putting it. I liked Clive Mailer. Liked him a lot."

"I'm listening."

"But I liked his wife even more."

"I see."

"No, you don't bloody well see, Sergeant." Bullock took a drink. "You don't see because you can't. Do you know where I was when I heard that he had fallen from that bloody mountain and broken every bone in his body?"

"Tell me."

40

"In bed with his wife. At lunchtime on Sunday! I'd been there since last night."

"I see." Hill felt a surge of sour disappointment. A man in bed at Pottersby could hardly be directly implicated in a fall from a cliff in Wales. But . . . dead man . . . wife playing up . . . there were the beginnings of a very familiar pattern here. Perhaps the skilled mathematician had found his own way of solving the eternal triangle.

"You see? You keep on saying you see. You don't at all. The phone on the bedside table rang. She answered it. It was Crome to tell her about Clive. Can you bloody well appreciate the situation? Think it through, Sergeant, and then you'll see what I mean. Another man's wife naked in your arms, mourning the imminent death of the husband she's just deceived. Not exactly the pleasantest way to end a dirty week-end, do you think?"

"Hardly."

"Now do you see why I'm going to get paralytic? Do you?"

Hill nodded. All he could think of to say was: "So you're not a mountaineer, Alec?"

The reply surprised him.

"Of course I bloody well am. Or was. I haven't been away with them on these Sunday jaunts for months now."

"Ah!" Hill thought he knew the reason. With Mailer a keen climber and, therefore, presumably away quite often at week-ends, Mrs Mailer would be free to entertain Bullock. His thoughts were interrupted by Bullock.

"Not what you're thinking, Sergeant. It wasn't because of Marian Mailer that I stopped climbing. I didn't get to . . . well, know her properly, until I started having every week-end free just like she did."

"Why did you stop going on the trips, then?"

"Because I'm gutless."

"You're what?"

"Scared."

"Of mountains?"

"Yes. I wasn't, until eight months ago. But about that time I nearly bought it. That did for me."

"You nearly fell?" Hill was now more interested than ever. Here was a scientist who had probably had the same experience as his three colleagues, but who had lived to tell the tale. The one who got away, in fact. He recalled Masters' reference to the possibility of three murders—or more.

"You slipped?"

"No, I didn't. Otherwise I shouldn't be here now probably. I got a dizzy spell. On a traverse. I was flat against the rock, leaning over sideways to the left when all of a sudden the whole blasted mountain started turning somersaults."

"You managed to hang on, though."

"Obviously. I'd tied on just a moment before and I'd got good holds for both hands and feet. Otherwise I'd have gone like a stone."

"It passed off quite quickly—the dizzy spell?"

"Did it hell! Not for several minutes after I'd taken a swig from my flask."

"Water?"

"Flask! Brandy!"

"Brandy? On a mountain?"

"I know what you're thinking. That I was drunk. I wasn't. I promise you I'd had nothing to drink except water from my bottle half an hour earlier. But I always carry a flask in my breast pocket. Just in case I'm caught out at night in an exposed place. By the grace of God I remembered I'd got it when the world started swimming. I just managed to get it out of my pocket with one hand. I tell you it saved my life. Three or four minutes after I'd had it, I began to recover. Another three or four minutes and I was able to start down."

"Completely recovered?"

"Badly shaken, I can tell you. I'd been going round on that pitch like a croupier's ball for nearly twenty minutes by my reckoning, and that's a hell of a time to defy gravity. I know it finished me as regards mountaineering."

"It's an interesting story, Alec."

"Meaning you don't believe me?" Bullock seemed to have

42

sobered up slightly, but his manner seemed to be growing belligerent.

"Meaning I believe every word you've told me. And I'm grateful you did tell me. Now, if you intend to go on drinking, I'll get you another."

"You'll join me?"

"I'd like to eat. But I tell you what I will do, tomorrow. And that's introduce you to Superintendent Masters, my boss. I think you'll like him. He's a bit of a clever devil, but he's an understanding bloke."

"George Masters?"

"That's the one. You've heard of him?"

"Who hasn't?"

Brant had got separated from Hill. As more people came into the bar, the two sergeants were nodded to or given good evening in a pleasant enough way. And just as Hill had become involved with Bullock, so Brant found himself talking to two young scientists. One male, one female.

Gerald Newsom—at Brant's best guess—was about twenty-seven. He was a pleasant-faced young man with a large moustache. Brant got the impression he had grown it in the vain hope of giving himself a little air of authority in this community where he appeared to be much the youngest. Unfortunately, as he drank, the beer froth adhered to the ends of the face fungus and made a ludicrous picture. But he was impeccably dressed in a charcoal-grey suit with limb-clinging trousers that showed off admirably the strength of his long legs.

"Astrology's the thing," said Newsom to Brant. "That'd solve your mystery for you. What the quasars foretell! Black holes of hell gape upon those born under the sign of the goat! I'm engaged in collecting every so-called forecast for every day and comparing them one with the other. I shall do it for a year and a day and publish my findings."

"So you're the one," said Cynthia Dexter, coming up behind him, with a glass of tomato juice.

"Of course I'm the one," said Newsom, turning towards her. "But which particular one did you mean?"

"The clot who cuts up all the papers in the ante room every day."

"I only cut out What The Stars Foretell columns. Don't tell me you read them."

"Unlike ninety per cent of other people, I'm a non-believer, but I do like a whole newspaper."

"If you want to see what you've missed, come up and see my scrapbook sometime."

"If I came near you it would be a scrap. For virtue." She smiled at Brant. "We're ignoring you and you're a guest here, aren't you? I heard somebody say you're a detective."

"Sergeant Brant, ma'am."

"And I'm Cynthia Dexter, usually referred to as Sin in the 'ugly-as' context. This, in case he hasn't told you, is Gerald Newsom, gently-bred, well-educated, beautifully-spoken, highly-connected and totally-useless."

"How d'you do, Mr Newsom."

"Oh, come on now, Sin. Play fair." He turned to Brant. "You can see how much store to set by what she says. When she calls herself as ugly as sin she lies in her teeth. Her veracity is equally at fault when describing me."

Brant could see the force of this argument clearly enough. Miss Dexter—at least he assumed she was not married because she wore no rings—was a personable woman, not much older than Newsom. She was long blonde, with beautiful regular teeth, all her own, the sort of lips that Brant imagined could smile while being kissed and eyes that had a twinkling humour much like a single expensive item in a diamond merchant's display.

"You don't have to worry," said Brant. "Either of you. I've been taught to take nothing I hear for granted, but to believe the evidence of my own eyes."

"A pretty speech," said Newsom. "It deserves more beer. Same again, Sergeant Brant?"

"Please."

Cynthia Dexter smiled at him. "Are all policemen like you?

You don't seem a bit like the archetype fuzz I heard so much about as a student."

"I don't suppose I am. And I've never met a copper who is—if you can believe that."

"I think I can."

"Would you like a cigarette?"

"Thank you." She accepted a light. "I suppose you're here because of Clive Mailer."

"Because he was the third scientist from here to die in the same way."

She looked at him gravely. "I've only been here just over a year, but I knew all three of them."

"Well?"

"Not awfully well. I never worked with any of them."

"Pity. You might have been able to tell me what it was in their characters that made Redruth and Mailer climb alone, when it's usual for climbers to rope together."

She frowned prettily. "I know why Philip Redruth did it. For a bet."

Brant felt vaguely excited. "What sort of a bet? Who with?"

"I honestly don't know—or if I ever did, I've forgotten."

"How did you hear about it?"

"I don't remember that, either. Perhaps I'm wrong. You'd better forget it or I'll be accused of misleading you—hampering the police in the course of their investigations is the term, isn't it?"

"Something like that. Oh, thank you." He took the tankard Newsom was holding out to him. "Cheers."

"What have you two been gassing about in my absence?"

"Mr Brant was asking if I knew why Philip Redruth and Clive Mailer should have gone on to the pitches alone."

Newsom shrugged. "I can't help you there. I'm not a mountaineer."

"Wouldn't your all-knowing stars help us?"

"Who can tell? The horoscopes of all three men. . . ."

"Oh, shut up! You're the horror, Gerald." She addressed both men. "Finish those drinks and let's eat."

"Not for me," said Newsom. "I'm due in the village to play bridge with the General."

"That's why you're all dressed up!" She turned to Brant. "One of his highly-placed distant relatives. They're spattered all over the land." She smiled. "It looks as though you're stuck with me for a supper partner, if you can bear the prospect."

Brant put his empty tankard on a nearby table. "I shall be delighted."

"Are all women as trusting as that with policemen?" asked Newsom.

"It's one of the few perks of the job," replied Brant. "Haven't you noticed that policemen's wives are always the best-looking girls around? It's a fact. Get to know a few some time."

When they were seated at table, Brant asked Cynthia: "*Is* Mr Newsom totally useless? I ask because you described him that way when introducing us, and it could be that with his connections he might get a job a bit above his ceiling."

Cynthia grinned delightedly. "Handsome, well-breeched Gerald isn't your idea of a serious-minded boffin, is that it?"

"He seemed a little . . . superficial, to me," admitted Brant. "Acts the fool a bit, I dare say."

"Don't let appearances mislead you, nice Mr Policeman. Gerald is a silly ass on the surface, but a resolute character inside. The point is that, unlike most of us here who have to scrabble for a foothold in science, he has never had to put up much of a fight for anything in his life. He was born nicely-thank-you in the social and financial senses, and he was endowed with enough grey matter to make full use of what he was born to. So he can't really imagine why anybody should get very intense about work—except when actually doing it. I suspect him, deep down, of being an ambitious scientist despite his amiable oaf antics."

"When you say ambitious, what exactly do you mean?"

Cynthia opened her eyes at that one.

"There are unsuspected depths to you, too, Mr Fuzz. That is, if I read your question aright. Do I?"

"I was always brought up to believe that everything is comparative," said Brant. He speared half a pickled onion and popped it into his mouth. "Lovely sweet violets you have here, Miss Dexter. One of my great weaknesses, sweet violets."

"Doesn't your wife object to your eating them at supper-time? Or does she take the line of least resistance and eat them, too, in sheer self-defence?"

"The girl that I marry," said Brant, not looking at her, "will have to be an onion-eater."

"You're not married? But I thought from the way you were running on about how good-looking police wives are that you would be hitched to a former Miss Spanish Onion circa nineteen seventy."

"As you so rightly said a moment or two ago, first impressions can be misleading. Up to now I am heart-whole and fancy onions."

"He would be humorous." Cynthia smiled. Brant found something special in that smile. He had to make a great mental effort to jerk himself back to reality and remind his companion that the conversation had strayed.

"Oh, yes! Everything is comparative. What about it?"

"As if you didn't know! Newsom's ambition. How shall I put it. . . ?"

"What you are asking me is whether Gerald is ambitious to become a leading light in his own right, or whether his ambition is simply to be on equal terms with his colleagues."

"That's right. I regard the one as a soaring ambition where one strives to stand out head and shoulders above one's work-mates—something like my boss, George Masters—the other as a rather comfortable posture which enables one to live on more or less equal professional terms with those around one—a situation in which their conversation is on one's own level, their—perhaps somewhat limited—goals one's own goals."

"I get your drift. I'll try to answer you despite the fact that you make the ordinary run of us poor scientists sound terribly smug and self-satisfied. Almost like bureaucrats for whom the future is already laid down and secure as long as we keep our noses clean and our superannuation subscriptions up."

"I didn't mean to . . ."

"Of course you didn't. I'm ribbing you because you've been a

47

clever Mr Plod. Gerald could never be one of the herd. Or at least not for long. I would say that ambition would drive him into becoming the government's senior scientific adviser. That would be the sort of mixture he would love—a nice corridor of power leading to his research lab."

"Would you say that on his way to his ultimate objective he would have a half-way mark? Somewhere where he might rest to recuperate for the final onslaught?"

"The second, more comfortable ambition you spoke of? Equality with his peers rather than superiority?"

"Yes."

"I think he might. Or he might appear to. Gerald would never want to give the impression that he was a professional rung higher. He would regard that as bad-mannered. But he would like the fact to be acknowledged by others, nonetheless."

"So you reckon he is a very determined young man." Brant was stating a conclusion, not asking a question. As he spoke, he realised with some amazement that in conversation with Cynthia Dexter he was reaching a standard of verbal exchange such as he had never achieved before. But he got little time to wonder why this was so before Cynthia continued.

"Gerald was born to regard the doing of a good job as the corner-stone of life, and he was blessed with enough brains to improve even on that precept."

"Thank you."

"Satisfied?" That smile again.

"Shall we just say better informed?"

"You've been using me, you have." There was no reproach in the tone.

"Were you ever in any doubt about that? I didn't try to hide the fact that I'm a policeman here on a job."

"You're frank, too. But I don't know that I like being used." This time she sounded a little more in earnest.

Brant put his knife and fork carefully on his empty plate. "When I admit to using you, I mean I am trying to get into the boffin mind, which is alien to me. I was not questioning you with the intention of trying to incriminate Mr Newsom."

48

"I should hope not. But when you discuss o'erweening ambition, you are touching on what may be regarded as motive for aberrant behaviour."

"True. And I confess that should any of us in the team find the slightest link between Mr Newsom and the three deaths, then I would use what you have told me without compunction—if I thought it relevant."

"I see."

"That's how you work, too, isn't it? You take everything into account when doing research."

"You are a clever Mr Flatfoot, you know. Turning every word said to your own advantage. I'd like to change the subject. What shall we talk about now?"

"You," said Brant. "I'd like to know a lot more about you."

"Professionally, or otherwise?"

"That," said Brant, "would be telling."

Green and Toinquet had returned to the bar after supper.

"Not bad beer this, Widow."

Toinquet grimaced. "I've always suspected these scientists of adding a flask of raw alcohol to every keg of beer that comes into the mess. Either that or the local brewery makes a special bevvy for them—as a sort of insurance against being blown up or polluted."

"Now there's a point. How does a security man like you make sure that what enters the Centre in the barrels is beer and nothing but beer?"

"We can't. Short of sampling it, there's no way. And if we sampled, my crew would be half seas over most of the time."

"Or dead from some noxious substance."

"There's always that."

"Could Mailer have been poisoned?"

"Ask me another. Post-mortems on the first two obviously showed no hint of poison in the systems, otherwise you'd have been here months ago. What Mailer's guts will show you'll know tomorrow or the next day."

"Why should he be such a BF as to climb alone?"

49

"We've answered that one."

"Not to my satisfaction you haven't, Widow. I can understand the first chap, Redruth, doing it, but not anybody else. Not after one fatal casualty."

"Silk was roped to a second man."

"A novice who couldn't hold him. What's his name, by the way?"

"Hawker. Doctor of Philosophy. Nuclear physicist. He's never been on a mountain since."

"And no wonder. We shall want to see him."

"Now?"

"You mean he's here?"

"About four feet behind you. From the looks of him he's only come in to get news of Mailer, and what he's heard seems to be bringing back unhappy memories."

"Is he drowning his sorrows?"

"In so far as he's not a great drinker but he's on his second sherry now, yes."

"Do you keep an eye on every tot that's drunk by this crowd?"

Toinquet closed one eye. "Unobtrusively. It's a good idea from the security angle. You know as well as I do, Greeny, that part of my job is to watch out for any habits—drinking, sexual, financial —that could put an employee here at risk from blackmail."

"Do you reckon Hawker would mind meeting me now? Or will my presence push him over the edge of grief to the point where he'll have to have a third sherry to sustain him?"

Toinquet took Green by the arm and turned him about. "Come on. He's alone at the moment."

"Doctor Tom Hawker: Detective Inspector Green of Scotland Yard."

Hawker was a big man. Green thought he was big enough to box in the dreadnought class—that was, if he could box. His hair was short, scrubby and indeterminate brown. The eyebrows were slightly darker, the eyes the colour of the bag-blue Green's mother used to use on washing day, the chin square and protuberant. He gave an immediate impression of great physical strength.

"Clive Mailer was a friend of mine," said Hawker. "A great

friend. We were at Cambridge together and then met up again here. We're near-neighbours in Pottersby. Can't you people stop these bloody mountains claiming victims like him—and Stanley Silk?"

"We're going to try, Doctor. But is it the mountains that claim them? Or is it some other agency? I know you can't answer that one, but as I've said, we're going to try to do so. We think our success will depend entirely on what sort of co-operation we get here in the Centre."

"What does that mean?"

"It means people have got to talk to us. Tell us everything they know and then some, so's we can fit it together to make sense. Then perhaps we'll get to know why these valuable lives have been lost and—equally important—how they were lost."

"And when you do get to know why and how, what then?"

"We can put a stop to whatever has caused it. For instance, Doctor, you were on that face or pitch or whatever it's called when Doctor Silk fell. What happened?"

"He fell."

"Now, now, Doctor, you know better than that. You conduct experiments, don't you? You don't just give the results. You make a note of every bit of apparatus you use, every step you take, every reading you make . . ."

"From the beginning, Tom," urged Toinquet. "Everything, right down to the colour of your socks."

Hawker put a hand to his brow, dug fingers into his eye-corners in an effort to remember and marshal the facts.

"We were to make an easy climb."

"Your first?"

"Yes. Stanley Silk had cajoled me into it. We stood at the bottom, among scree and loose rocks, and Stan gave me my instructions. I can remember him saying that it was a very easy first pitch, but it looked pretty fearsome to me. He laughed when I said so. Told me that if I wanted a final nervous pee, then was the time to have it, or if my mouth was dry, then was the time to have a last swig at the water bottle."

"And did you?"

"What? Oh, yes. I went behind a rock—there were some of the women walkers nearby."

"Drink?"

"Yes, I think so."

"What about Silk?"

"He did the same. I can remember thinking that for an expert who wasn't nervous at the thought of the climb he showed as much strain as I did. He joined me behind the rock and then had a good long gulp of water, and away we went."

"Roped together?"

"Just like the book says you should be. He went first and I payed out. He was pretty quick and he kept calling out to me exactly what he was doing and where I'd find holds. He told me I should have no difficulty because the pitch had been climbed so many times before there were easily recognisable marks all the way up and all the loose earth and stones had been scrabbled out of the nicks and off the ledges so nothing should give way under my weight."

"How far up did he go before you started?"

"About sixty feet, I think. He wanted a good spot because although it had only taken him a few minutes to get up there, he knew I'd take much longer and he wanted an easy wait."

"But you managed it eventually?"

"Oh, yes. It was much easier than I'd feared it might be—due to Stan's instructions and his hand on the rope, of course. Then, when I reached him, he led off again."

"Leaving you on the easy ledge he'd selected."

"He called it easy. I didn't. I found it hell's own delight just hanging on there. I hadn't enough hands to cling tightly and pay out the rope."

"So what happened?"

"He was making for a spot just about a hundred feet above us and slightly to our right. He said it was in the very easy class with nothing to test us except a very easy traverse about thirty feet up."

"He meant a move across the face of the climb?"

"So little it wasn't much more than a lean across, if you understand me. But he wanted to be sure he had enough rope and that

52

I didn't hamper him by not paying out as quickly as he liked—or at all. I told you I was clinging on like grim death."

"So what happened?"

"Before setting off he pulled out as much rope as he felt he would need—to relieve me of the job."

"Enough to reach the traverse thirty feet up, or the ledge a hundred feet up?"

"Whichever it was to have been, he made a mistake. Too much for the traverse, too little for the ledge. Anyhow, he didn't think he needed to secure it before the traverse. He told me he would put something in—he was carrying channel pitons and bolts—on both sides of the traverse to make it easy for me."

"But he fell before he could rope on?"

"He was left-handed, you see. And as I remember it, he leaned over to get a good grip out on his right and to leave his left hand free to fix the piton. He was in the act of doing it when he fell."

"You couldn't hold him?"

"I could have done, if he hadn't had so much rope. I could have taken his weight somehow and held on, but he'd got about seventy feet looped behind him—more than the distance I was up from the scree and loose rocks. Before I could get in the slack he'd hit the bottom."

"How did he fall? Did his foot slip? Rock give way? Hand lose its hold?"

"As far as I could see it was none of those. I have a dim recollection of him shaking his head, and I thought he must have got dust or earth on his face and was trying to shake it off."

"Did you call out to him?"

"No. I thought it better not to. I didn't want to distract him."

"How long did this head-shaking last?"

"It seemed like an age at the time. Probably thirty or forty seconds."

"Did he then try to fix the piton?"

"He certainly stretched out his left arm and he had the piton in his hand, but I got the impression that it was something of an act of desperation."

"Could you explain that a bit more fully, Doctor?"

"Well, you know if you get soap in your eyes when washing, it hurts like hell. You shut your eyes tight, screw up your face and feel for the towel. You know you won't get any relief until you do get the towel and clap it to your face and wipe away the suds."

"Something of that sort happened to Silk?"

"I thought so. Mind you, I was looking almost vertically upwards, so I couldn't really see his face. But I think he had his eyes shut and he was fumbling desperately to get the piton in before he sneezed or something like that. I felt he needed to place the piton and get a grip of it before he could breathe freely again."

"But he failed?"

"He fell all of a piece. Every hold went together. No lingering, hanging on by one hand, fingers slipping. No scrabbling with the feet. He just came away like a sack of spuds. No warning to me. Nothing."

"Suicide, perhaps?"

"Stanley Silk? Suicide? No, Inspector. Never."

"How long did all this take?"

"From Silk leaving the ground to his falling? Less than forty minutes. About thirty-seven. It was all worked out at the time."

"And then you had to get down by yourself."

"I managed it. As I said, it was well marked and I'm big enough to reach holds a little too far out for some men."

"And when you got to the bottom you had to deal with Silk."

"Not directly. There was a sort of base camp there with one or two of our people around. They'd naturally gone to him when he fell. He was dead, I believe, when they reached him. By the time I got down somebody had set off to call an ambulance."

"Thank you, Dr Hawker. You've been a great help."

"I don't see how."

Toinquet patted him on the arm. "All information is useful in an investigation, Tom. Even if it's negative it can help to show that there is no common pattern in the three falls, for instance."

"Oh, in that case . . . no, thanks, I'll not have another drink. I must get off home."

Chapter 3

It was after nine o'clock by the time Masters had rounded up his team for a conference in his room. Brant and Hill fetched chairs from their own rooms. The brown rep curtains were pulled together. Cigarettes and Masters' pipe were lit. The air grew blue and then fetid. And they talked. Each reported—as near verbatim as makes no matter—to the others, so that all were informed. It was almost eleven when Brant, who had spoken last, finished.

Masters filled and lit his pipe for the third time.

"In view of the opinions expressed in the car on the way down here, I think you've all done a remarkably good job in a short space of time. While it's too early to congratulate ourselves, I feel that if we stick to it at this rate, we could begin to get somewhere within the foreseeable future. Does anybody feel that I am being too optimistic?"

"Yes," said Green who was sprawled on the bed. "We could fill the *Encyclopaedia Britannica* with reports like this and still fail."

"Agreed. Without the vital spark to light the fire. But at any rate we're gathering plenty of fuel."

Green gestured his assent. "We've found out that these boffins like to talk, and I didn't expect that."

"It also shows they've got pretty good memories," said Hill. "Not the absent-minded type."

"OK," said Green. "So I said they would be. But let's not start jumping with glee. We've got a bit of something to work on, but we're still a long way from home. Anybody got a fag? I seem to have lost mine."

"Smoked them all, you mean," said Brant, handing him a packet. "Keep it. You'll not get any more before morning."

"Suspects," said Masters. "Who have we got so far?"

"You're going to discuss them as suspects this early in the case, Chief?" asked Hill.

"Why not? These aren't cosh merchants, you know. Not Bovver Boys. Motive—other than pure thuggery—is going to be important. But it's hidden. We'll have to speculate to stumble on it."

"You reckon?" asked Green. "I mean, there's old Widow Twankey out there as nervous as a half-set jelly, but I can't see him as the murderer."

"Why not?" asked Brant.

"I'd quite like him to be," admitted Green. "But that's because I've never taken a shine to him."

"More than that," suggested Masters. "Positive dislike, I'd have said."

"You're right. He's mean. He always has been. Probably he's a better Security buff because of it. I don't know. But I do know he's hiding something. . . ."

"A lot of them may be," interposed Hill.

"Maybe, lad. But Widow's Security. Almost one of us, not one of your snot-filled boffins. He should be co-operating at top level."

"If he isn't, doesn't that automatically make him suspect?"

"Of being guilty of something? Sure."

"Put it this way," said Hill. "If we're up against a conspiracy . . ."

"Oh, blimey!"

"We could be. More than one of them in cahoots. Couldn't Toinquet be an active member?"

"More likely to be an accessory before or after," said Masters. "Knows something rather than being an actual member of a conspiracy."

"Right, Chief. Either way he'd be guilty. If the DI is right— and there's no reason to suppose he's not—Toinquet's holding out on us. The hallmark of the accessory—yes? Conspiracy of silence, if you like. But equally guilty."

"I told him we'd be leaning on him," said Green.

"You did what?"

"Don't sound so scandalised, Sergeant. I wanted to scare him."

"Into doing or saying something to give himself away?"

"That's right."

"That's the ... what d'you call it, Chief? ... of how to interrogate witnesses—to frighten them."

"Antithesis? Agreed—at any time but this. I think the DI is entitled to put pressure on to a Security man where it would be unforgiveable in the case of other witnesses. And don't forget the DI was not interrogating him officially—merely talking to him."

"And having put the shakes up him," said Green, "we've now got to watch him like sailors watching a strip act. There's no good getting him to give himself away and not being in the audience to see what he does."

"So he is definitely a suspect?" asked Brant.

Masters nodded.

"Who else, Chief?"

"What about Crome?" asked Green. "Or is the big boss out of the running just because he is the big boss?"

"Nobody's above suspicion," replied Masters. "It appears, as I've already told you, that the scandal of a triple murder investigation could do him a lot of harm politically and professionally, so on the principle that he has most to lose, one could suggest that he wouldn't do anything as stupid as murder to jeopardise his career. But scientists of his calibre are people who weigh evidence just as much as we do. It is possible to suppose that Crome— faced with a choice of two evils—may have weighed the two factors one against the other and decided that murder was likely to be the lesser."

"I don't get it," said Hill.

"Oh, come on now," said Green. "Crome's a top dog. Say he got to the top through doing some scientific research which he fudged but got accepted. Then there comes along a bright boyo who sees through Crome's fudge and is prepared to blow the gaff. What's Crome's position? If he does nothing he's shown up as a fraud and loses his job. But if the bright boyo can be disposed of before he can spill the beans, then Crome will still be Director and not a disgraced has-been."

"I see. But would he chop three of them?"

"I don't know, do I? But if that were the position, it could be that every so often the fudge would be discovered by another bright boyo. If so—three deaths."

"You mean it would go on for ever?"

"Not necessarily—or Crome may think not. He could be working like hell to produce the real McCoy. Once he succeeds, he can turn round and apologise for making a mistake in the first project. Then he can add that it was a lucky mistake, after all, because it has led to this better discovery he has found. When that happens, he won't have to knock off anybody else and he'll be as safe as houses in his job. But the point of the argument is that he will have weighed the relative risks of committing murder against those of losing his reputation. And he has decided he is clever enough to get away with murder—as he has done. Nobody suspected him the first time or the second. So . . ." Green sat up and stubbed out his cigarette. "So, he had a third bash when the need arose. Unluckily for him, this time, Whitehall sticks its nose in."

"Is that what you had in mind, Chief?"

"More or less. If needs be, I could support what the DI has said with a few more observations. Why didn't Crome call us in off his own bat? Why didn't he take some action after the second death? Why, despite protests from the Security man, did he insist on Toinquet being present at our first meeting? To protect him—under the guise of security—from saying things he shouldn't? If it comes to that, why did Toinquet prefer not to stay? I find that odd. I'd have thought that normally he would have been agog to hear all that was to be said. But did he want to leave because he knew something he didn't want to be surprised into revealing? Something about the Director? Why did Crome cut such an important meeting short? Was there some important matter he had to attend to before we could come across it? And so on, and so on."

Hill said, "It would make a nice case, Chief. But are you seriously suggesting that Crome may have acted in this way?"

"Do you seriously suggest that we should overlook him?"

"No. But that fairy story . . ."

"I'm not asking you to accept it as told. Nor is the DI. He merely illustrated what I was attempting to convey, and that is that a cool, calculating brain may weigh two courses of action—one of which may be murder—and come to a conscious decision to avoid the one which promises immediate professional repercussions in the hope of gaining enough time to save the day in some other way."

"Right, Chief. Anybody else?"

Brant said: "Gerald Newsom."

"Not your little girl scientist?" sneered Green.

"Maybe. But not just yet, I think."

"Not even if she made up that story about that bet?"

"Let's try Newsom," said Masters. "As I see him—after hearing your report—this Newsom chap appears to make a lot of hay with words which are apparently unsupported by thought. But Miss Dexter has warned us not to be fooled. She says there is hidden purpose in Newsom. So, Sergeant, you winkled out the story; now you can give us an opinion."

Brant flexed both arms. "Can I be as far-fetched as the DI, Chief?"

"What's good for the goose . . ."

"Well then, Newsom is interested in astrology. Now that makes me think a bit. A pure scientist dabbling in predictions—and not even the pseudo-scientific side of prognostication . . ."

"Meaning?" asked Green.

"The real astrology buffs work pseudo-scientifically from carefully prepared charts. So even if the basis on which they work is a load of rubbish, at least they use some semblance of learning in producing their results. But Newsom is apparently trying to collate all the various daily paper forecasts. I can't believe that even astrologers are very serious about those. I mean, think what is being offered. One in every twelve people has exactly the same forecast in any given paper. That's bad enough. But there are scores of magazines and papers all producing entirely different forecasts supposedly covering each of those twelve groups for exactly the same times. I reckon that any scientist who's trying to make sense of that lot is either a fool or he's trying something on. And Newsom, by all reports, is no fool."

"Goody, goody," said Green. "What's he trying?"

Masters interrupted. "Don't forget he may be trying to show just how absurd is the widespread belief in what the stars foretell. That could be a worthwhile debunking project in his eyes."

"I'd thought of that," admitted Brant. "A really properly written, scientific study to explode the myth may have struck Newsom as a good idea. It's the sort of publication which could well attract a lot of popular attention. That would get Newsom's name in lights without his treading on any scientific toes in the process. And it wouldn't destroy his silly-ass image if, as I guess, he wears it to cloak the iron purpose underneath. What better way to get topsides with his colleagues than a popular paper with which no true scientist would disagree?"

"Good point," growled Green, slipping his legs to the floor. "I'm going for a jimmy, not having been born under the sign of Aquarius the water carrier."

"Carry on," said Masters after this interruption. "That is, if you intend to disregard what you have just said and produce some arcane motive for Newsom's activities.

"I have to, Chief. If his paper is really going to be a scientific debunking of astrology, we can't include him on the list of suspects. But he may have an ulterior motive—bearing in mind he's an ambitious man. Ambition often seeks to remove anything or anybody standing in its way."

"True. You think Silk, Redruth and Mailer could have been on the rungs of the ladder just above Newsom?"

"As to that, Chief, I can't say. But I wouldn't have thought that top scientists were so thick on the ground that getting rid of three or four of them wouldn't thin the field considerably."

Green returned. "You reckon he did knock 'em off, do you?"

"For the purposes of this discussion I am assuming so."

"How? He's not a mountaineer."

"Couldn't that be a point in favour of suspecting him? Nobody was near any of those three men when they fell, so why does it have to be a mountaineer who culled them? Couldn't we be meant to look hard at the climbing fraternity and disregard the non-climbers?"

"Point taken. Are you going to give him a motive?"

"Turn what I've said about the paper he's preparing about face. If a debunking report would gain a lot of publicity, think how much more a really serious, scientific study supporting astrology would attract."

"I don't get it," said Green. "You're wanting it both ways."

"Am I? Scientific papers are based on facts and case histories and so on. Say Newsom was able to prove that certain horoscopes foretold a sticky end for certain people, and those people were *actually* cut off in their prime. Think of the sensation that would cause."

"One moment," said Masters. "Is your point that Newsom has prepared horoscopes for everybody in Pottersby—secretly, of course—and then actually caused to happen what he had worked out?"

"In three specific and dramatic instances, yes, Chief. He may have tried it on others—on Bullock, for instance. When he found a horoscope which indicated that the owner was scheduled for untimely death, he decided to make the prediction happen. He found a way of doing it among mountaineers. He succeeded three times and failed at least once and, as far as we know, hasn't got round to operating on non-climbers yet. But you must admit it would add a bit of spice to a report."

"This," said Green, "beats the band. I said we'd need to know the second law of thermodynamics to crack this case. I was wrong. We need to know the planets and their movements."

"The big thing," said Masters, "would seem to be to discover whether any or all of our three victims had the dread malefics at the wrong places in their charts."

"Mally who?"

"Baleful stellar influences—one of the jargon words of the cult."

"Oh, is it? And which of us is going to decide if they had or not?"

"None of us," said Masters. "And I'll tell you why. One point

I can't get out of my mind is that the three dead men all came from the same group. It would be too much of a further coincidence to believe that star charts would pick out three victims so closely linked by circumstances. So I'm not prepared to waste time on learning birth times—actual or sidereal—and discovering which planets exerted an influence on those three lives—not yet, at any rate. If we have to do so later, so be it. We'll get an expert who can read houses and sign/planet relationships."

"So we disregard Newsom."

"No. If he's our man, he'll offer us much more material motives than those from ephemeris. That's what we need. I don't fancy going into a witness box to answer questions on the zodiac and astrological tables."

Green grunted assent.

"After all," said Masters, "we've got lots to work on. DI Green got an eye-witness account of one of the falls. Several things spring to mind there. First, to get a second account of the same fall from somebody who was in the base camp and compare the two. Second, try to get eye-witness accounts of the other two falls for comparison. Third, get lists of the people in the base camps each time—if that was the usual way they played things."

"And lists of the people on the trips from Widow Twankey," added Green.

"Agreed. Can you and Hill start on those items tomorrow? Brant, I want you to chase up this wager your woman doctor was on about. Cultivate her a lot more. She may be able to introduce you to some useful contacts."

"Right, Chief."

"What are you going to do?" asked Green.

"Me?" asked Masters. "I'm going to turn nuclear physicist and sniff around the labs. I also want to get hold of all the medical evidence. We've got to drive this one on a loose rein. My feeling is there's something intrinsically wrong here. But I'll admit that there's probably something wrong in any closed community such as this. You can't box-up hundreds of egg-heads and not get animosities flaring and fits of tantrums sparking off all the time. And it may simply be some of these relatively minor conflicts that are causing my nose to twitch. But it could be the big thing, and that's what we're here to discover—if it exists."

"Widow Twankey thinks it doesn't."

"But according to your version of his conversation, he said he was going to call us in."

"He talks as he warms. I'm talking about what he thinks, not what he said."

"Are you sure?"

"He was putting up an umbrella for himself when he said he would have asked for us. But this is his patch. He doesn't want anything to be wrong."

"Reasonable enough," said Hill. "But I wonder if he knew Alec Bullock was having it off with Mrs Mailer?"

"Why should he?"

"He gives me the impression he thinks he knows everything that goes on here. If he could miss that little bit of scandal it could be that he misses quite a lot of other things. Like Alec Bullock nearly being a fourth faller."

"See what you mean," said Green. "We can trust Widow's lists and any other bureaucratic information he's got, but we can't rely on him for pay dirt. I'm agreeing with you."

"That seems reasonable," said Masters. "For instance, I notice that they have public call-booths in the corridor outside the mess. Anybody here can bypass the Centre's switchboard."

"People must be allowed to make a private call. And if they couldn't do it inside the compound, they'd do it outside."

"Quite. But it is still a loophole which Toinquet could not hope to plug unless he has wire-tappers and recorders attached to each one. It merely illustrates how difficult total security is to achieve." Masters got to his feet and stretched. "Right. That's enough for tonight."

Green yawned openly. "Time for kip in my little barrack bed. I wonder if they'll give us boiled liver for breakfast like they used to sometimes in the army?"

Hill shuddered realistically.

"Good, it was, son. With little bits of onion floating in the jizzer-rizzer. Used to mop it up with that purple bread we got in those days. Just the job at half-six in the morning when snow was on the ground."

"Get out," ordered Masters. "The lot of you. And thank heaven for Mister Kellogg before you go to sleep."

Chapter 4

"I THOUGHT I'D take you round myself," said Crome.
The Director had come into the dining room and stopped by
Masters' chair just as the Superintendent was finishing breakfast.
"That is, if you want to visit the laboratories."

"I was intending to visit Group Six," admitted Masters. "Just
me. Not the whole crowd of us."

Crome sat down. Masters noted the strain in his eyes—far
greater than the evening before—and diagnosed a sleepless night.
He wondered why. Offhand he could think of two reasons. The
first, that though he was trying to play it cool, Crome felt himself
tremendously involved in this investigation. Probably he had at
last realised how much the tragedy and the inevitable scandal
could affect his own career. The second was equally obvious:
guilt. A man with a conscience, Masters knew, can screw himself
up to the point where he will take a certain course of action and,
even when it has been completed, still believe it to have been the
right course. But conscience is subject to neither rhyme nor reason.
Once roused, it becomes the ever-present voice of condemnation,
fostering mental unease. It dispels sleep and quietness of mind,
even if it does not always make a coward of its host. Whichever
of the two reasons was the one which was now occupying the
scientist's mind, it was this, Masters guessed, which had driven
him to leave his own flat in the main house to come over to the
mess so early on a Monday morning to see for himself what the
Yard team was planning. The offer of a conducted tour coming
from so busy a man could only be an excuse for activity dictated
by worry.

"Just you? What are your colleagues doing?"

"This and that. Getting to know who was present when each

of your men was killed. That sort of thing." Masters got to his feet. "Ready when you are, Director."

"It's a quarter of a mile to the Group Six laboratory. Shall I get a car? Or do you mind walking?"

"I'd like to walk."

Masters guessed that Crome wished to talk as well as walk. When they left the mess building and started on a path which led across the grounds he was proved right.

"I hear you are a very successful detective, Mr Masters."

"As you've obviously been checking up on me, Director, there's little point in a show of mock modesty on my part."

Crome reddened. "It seemed right to me to know the type of man with whom I was dealing."

"Don't apologise. Making enquiries about people one comes into business contact with is an unexceptional, everyday precaution many of us take."

"That sounds as if you've been checking up on me."

"Could I do otherwise, Director? But I promise you this. I don't know if you're married, have a family, the state of your bank balance, your political leanings, the state of your health, or any of those things which either do not concern me or are irrelevant as far as this case is concerned."

"Thank you for that at any rate. But I was saying that you are, by reputation, a man who completes enquiries successfully. By that, I mean, neatly, cleanly and quickly. I am praying for your success here, but I confess to being nervous of it."

"Please tell me why."

"Because I think I could undergo a breach of security here without it affecting me as a person. It would be a thing apart from me. But the idea that murder literally stalks these compounds for which I am responsible; that at least one of my colleagues is homicidal; and that three of my staff have already been killed—well that doesn't leave me unmoved. Already, in my imagination, I am seeing horror."

"Director, it would be impertinent of me to tell you not to worry. But I feel I must just say that the mind is unpredictable. As a scientist, you know that only too well. And all the minds in this place are extraordinary—they're sharper and more carefully balanced than those in an average cross-section of people. Unpredictable means incapable of being forecast—and that applies to ordinary men and women. Extraordinary means out of the usual course. So when one of the great minds among your colleagues does go slightly off balance, the effects are likely to be surprisingly difficult to prophesy. But you must grasp the fact that, as like as not, there is no consciousness of great evil in this mind. It is probably adhering strictly to the logic that training and experience have imposed upon it. In other words, your attitude—until you know different—should be that one of these clever minds has gone a little too far in—shall we say—removing obstacles from its path. The pity is the obstacles were human beings."

"What you are saying is that the crime is merely one of degree."

"Only in so far as the guilty person is concerned. Not, of course, to the families and friends of the dead men, nor to me as the policeman faced with the job of resolving the problem."

"Where does that leave me?"

"Accepting that a mind has run off the rails. Accepting it logically if superficially. Sorrow for a short time if you must. Be on your guard for the future. Be aware of the signs that indicate such a thing might happen again. But don't let this diminish you personally."

"Thank you."

"As for the handling of the matter, I promise you it will be done as circumspectly as possible."

They walked on in silence for a moment or two. The morning was still grey, but the cold wind had dropped considerably. The temperature was comfortable for their exercise. But in Masters' mind there was just a nag of discomfort. He was wondering, somewhat guiltily, whether he had not gone a little further than wisdom dictated in speaking in this fashion to Crome. It was one thing to offer seemingly experienced—if banal—comfort and advice to the Director, but it was an entirely different matter if, in doing so, he had given the impression that Crome himself was regarded as above suspicion. It was a private rule in the Masters code that no suspect should ever knowingly be lulled into a belief of total security until this was proven. For Masters, there was something infinitely distasteful in the thought of incriminating a man who, until the moment he was taken, *knew* himself to be safe, and so was off-guard mentally as well as physically when that moment came. That he, himself, should be the reason for such assurance on the part of a suspect was anathema to him. He would prefer—like Green with Toinquet—to give the impression that he was looking harder at a suspect than was in fact the case—rather than the reverse. He was wondering exactly what to say to dispel all doubt and set the record straight when Crome reopened the conversation.

"I didn't expect you to regard your case in this way, Superintendent."

"Is there another way?"

"I expected your investigation to be heavy-handed. Not because I thought either you or your colleagues would be particularly ham-fisted, but because it is simply another job to you."

"True enough, Director. But it is an unusual job. Don't they say, these days, that get a man off the production line where every movement is the same, day in, day out, and put him on to a succession of jobs with variety and you increase his interest, his output, and the quality of his work?"

"How exactly do you work in order to maintain interest and increase variety?" asked Crome. "I'm asking because, judging by what you say, you policemen must have much in common with us scientists."

"Except that we usually have a body first," replied Masters drily. "You don't have any such tangible and urgent goal towards which to direct your research."

"Sometimes we do. Some of our opportunity targets are very urgent indeed, and not every project is open-ended. And even if there is no specific goal, we lay down a protocol—a record of the propositions agreed before we start work. Directives within groups spring from such protocols. Thereafter there may be a certain licence—a liberty of action conceded to each researcher, but only in order to try to make sure that unexpected opportunities shall not be lost."

"We are less formal, Director. We cast around much more. Within limits, of course, but even those are elastic."

"How do you cast? Planned sweep and search procedure?"

"Each case varies."

"This time? Here, where you are not absolutely sure you have a case to investigate and—supposing you are satisfied you have—there are possibly hundreds of suspects?"

"We talk to people. As I'm talking to you now. Making no effort to disguise the fact that we are sniffing around for a scent. We get the background and we try to find inconsistencies."

"It must be very difficult. One of your team hears some minute fact which—though he does not realise it—may be inconsistent with an equally minute fact heard by another. How do you marry them up for comparison? By the written word? So much of a conversation—nuances and emphases—must be missed if committed subsequently to paper."

Masters smiled. "I had a brain-storming session last night which lasted into the early hours."

"Brain storms are usually recorded."

"Not mine. We don't allow the sessions to spill over into total irrelevancies as per the book. We keep our eye on the goal. But we do have flights of fancy which spark ideas in others. Fortunately my people have good memories, so, as I said, we don't record."

"Have they near total recall?"

"At certain times. A built-in tape recorder that switches itself on when the policeman's special instinct whispers the word 'important'. It is not absolutely infallible, but it serves very well in a surprisingly high number of cases."

Crome smiled in a tired fashion. "You're refreshing to have around, Mr Masters. If we take this little path it leads us to the Group Six door. They share this complex with Groups Two and Seven both of which need certain services common to all three. Each has its own private door so that we can isolate one part if needs be."

"For security reasons?"

"Mainly. At its simplest it means that if one group wishes to work late the other areas can be locked up. But safety also comes into it."

"Does Toinquet keep a custodian permanently in the complex?"

"Three. But it's like gardening. If you plant nothing but roses in your flower beds you know that everything else that comes up is a weed. We report every lab closed when it is unoccupied. Any activity in it thereafter must be suspect."

"And how is suspicious activity—should there be any—discovered?"

"All the usual means. Close-circuit TV, magic eyes, alarm systems, time locks. Whatever the security people think up, we install. I think there are so many systems that anybody wishing to enter would be exercised in cutting out all the mechanical and electronic safeguards—all of which are fail-alarm. Then there are human guards and dogs."

"In other words, neither you nor Toinquet are likely to have any security worries which could stem from a break-in."

"None whatever. Short of an armed raid by a considerable number of highly trained men, we reckon we are safe in that respect."

Masters made no comment. He knew that the loophole which could not be plugged was the open mouth with the wagging tongue behind it. Nobody had yet managed to padlock that. When this thought struck him, he was inclined to offer up a little prayer of thanks. Still tongues were of no help to him.

When they arrived in the lobby of the complex, they were booked in by the custodian. Masters looked about him. The building was as strong as a pill box. Ultra modern; ultra clean. The floors shone; the paintwork glistened. The bullet-proof glass in the windows sparkled. Swinging fire-doors of polished mahogany with narrow peep-holes of wire-reinforced glass were everywhere.

"Where is Doctor Winter, please?"

The uniformed man replied that there was a Group meeting in Winter's office, called to redistribute the workload because of Mailer's death.

"Please don't interrupt it," said Masters.

"As you wish."

"There's a couple of chairs in the alcove, Director," said the custodian. "If you want to wait."

"Thank you. Please let Dr Winter know we are here and would like to see him when his conference ends."

They rounded a baffle wall and found the two chairs, a coffee table and a few magazines. As they sat down, Masters said, "My visit here is entirely in the pursuance of the job I have in hand. What I mean is, I haven't come to rubber-neck, nor do I want blinding with science—literally."

"I'm afraid that unless you are adamant—demand that your conversations shall be conducted in words of one syllable—you can't hope to escape the jargon and the enthusiasm which will drive these people into lengthy and—to the layman—incomprehensible diatribes concerning their work."

"What about you, Director? Can you tell me what goes on without confusing me?"

"I can try. Do you know anything of nuclear physics?"

"So little that you must assume I know nothing of it."

"As you wish. I told you last night that Group Six is engaged on tests concerning the shielding of small, tactical nuclear reactors."

"For driving boats and aircraft?"

"It's important—the world energy situation being what it is. Some people—particularly the Americans—are beginning to champion the use of hydrogen for aircraft fuel."

"Wouldn't that be highly dangerous? Hydrogen, I thought, is highly explosive. Wasn't it used in the gas bags of some of the airships, with disastrous results?"

"It was, indeed. But the amazing thing is it is no more likely to explode than some of the liquid fuels that the States use in jets—liquids that we over here don't like at all, although we had to use them on occasion when the fuel situation was desperate. No, the protagonists believe that if you can get your hydrogen out of a flimsy gas bag and into a pretty solidly built fuel tank, you'll be quite safe."

"You sound as if you disapprove of the scheme."

"I feel that our job as scientists is to come up with solutions

71

which will not saddle the man-in-the-street with a large financial burden nor spoil his countryside for him. . . ."

"Nor necessitate the building of plant which can blow up with devastating effect if a spark gets near some volatile substance."

"Quite. Now, in theory, this hydrogen scheme should be relatively cheap, in that water—and there's plenty of it in the seas —is two-thirds, in volume, hydrogen. All one has to do is extract it. A relatively easy process. And remember that when hydrogen burns as a fuel, it combines with oxygen in the air to revert back to water."

"But?"

"First off, the amount needed would pose tremendous problems. One would have to use nuclear power to produce it, and the question of storage would be almost insuperable. It has been estimated that we should need half a million tons a year. Half a million tons of the lightest substance known!"

"Wasn't coal gas largely hydrogen?"

"To be sure. Carburreted hydrogen. But can we honestly ring Heathrow with giant gasometers?"

Masters shuddered mentally at the thought: the eyesore, the danger, the navigational difficulties, and much more which even he could envisage.

"So you're looking for a way to make the provision of small nuclear reactors a feasible proposition?"

"That's it. As you must know, the rays or particles given off by uranium—particularly the Gamma rays—are lethal. The particles excite each other. Uranium atoms split—fission reaction. They excite each other again, they reach critical level and grow in intensity. All very dangerous. They must be shielded by dense material to prevent escape. So far, lead has always been used. We're trying an alternative dense shield—deuterium oxide."

"I see," said Masters gravely.

"You know what deuterium oxide is?" asked Crome with a grin.

"No, I can't say I do."

"To you—heavy water."

"Ah!"

72

"That rings a bell?"

"Of Commando raids on heavy water plant in Norway during the war. I've read of them."

"I guessed that was it. Deuterium is the mass two isotope of hydrogen. Symbol H two or D. When it collects some oxygen it becomes heavy water, and it's not difficult to make, nor is it rare in nature."

"No?"

"It is thought that in ordinary drinking water there are often particles of heavy water."

"You surprise me."

"I thought I would."

"A question, if I may. Who is responsible for handing each Group its brief or protocol or whatever instructions they receive for directing their research?"

"I am. But I try not to lay down the law so narrowly as to inhibit the natural inventiveness of the staff. And, of course, my directives for any project are never issued before discussion with the scientist who heads up the team."

"In this case, Doctor Winter. How old is he?"

"Over fifty."

"Why is he still here in the second league at his age?"

Crome shrugged. "Some say a scientist is at his creative best in his thirties."

"Could it be that he is not so outstanding a scientist as some of his subordinates are or have been?"

"That is very true. Several men from his group have been moved on."

"And up?"

Crome nodded. "But Winter is a solid man. I can best describe him as probably the ideal type of scientist to head up a workaday group in a place like Pottersby. He will never indulge his own flights of fancy because, able scientist though he is, he lacks the vital creative spark that the great innovator must have. But he will nurture creative talent in others. Am I giving you a picture you can recognise, Mr Masters?"

"I think so. I imagine he is the equivalent of what is known

73

in industry as a line extension man or, if you prefer it, the D half of R and D. Once the initial research is done he can cope quite adequately with the development side of things."

"I don't think I can better that as a superficial description of Winter—so long as you bear in mind that he has, when all's said and done, a vast amount of personal knowledge and talent."

"How successful has his particular piece of current research been up to date?"

"Don't think me equivocal, Mr Masters, but success in research can be positive or negative. You may not be quite so happy with negative results, but at least they tell you what you *can't* do, even if you don't learn what you *can* do."

"I have much the same experience—frequently," said Masters. "The negative side often serves to eliminate suspects, and so helps me considerably."

"My best reply to your question is, then, that we are progressing slowly. There's been eighteen months' work done on this project."

"A fleabite in research time, I suppose?"

Crome grinned. "The bible would call it less than the twinkling of an eye."

"No chance of a little fortuitous serendipity?"

This time Crome laughed aloud. "Serendipity is literally a fairy tale in our sphere. Horace Walpole coined the word after a fairy tale, and the faculty of making happy and unexpected discoveries by accident in nuclear physics is fairy-tale stuff."

"I've sometimes done it," murmured Masters.

"Because you're dealing with humans who, as you rightly pointed out a few minutes ago, are capable of any action. They are distinguished from everything else in the universe by the possession of free will. Nuclear particles behave in a predetermined pattern. And that pattern is like a child's toy compared with the innumerable capabilities of the human brain. Somewhere along the line one brain will make an abnormal move due to expectations preconditioned by previous acts. Your brain can note it—be it word or gesture. You have the ability to seize on to it, recognise it, place it and use it. This is what makes you a good detective."

Masters didn't reply. There was no reply that sprang readily to a mind already preoccupied with the thought that Crome would make a pretty tough adversary for a detective. A man with the mind not only of a top-grade scientist, but that of a philosopher, too. He understood what made a detective tick. The exact mechanical method of working was probably not known to him —as shown by his earlier questions—but such details were immaterial when he was capable of empathy on such a mental scale as he was now showing. Masters—not for the first time—wondered about Crome and braced himself to produce—much as lower-grade soccer sides are popularly supposed to do when faced by superior-grade opposition—his best form.

His thoughts were interrupted by a phone bell which rang outside the little alcove where they were sitting. They heard a murmur of voices and a few seconds later the custodian poked his head round the partition.

"Doctor Winter has finished his conference, Director. He's coming to collect you."

Crome got to his feet. Masters followed him into the vestibule.

"While you're here, Director, sir," said the custodian, "would you like a ticket in the sweep?"

"Which one is this?"

"National, sir."

"So early? There must be weeks to go."

"It takes weeks to get round this lot, sir."

"I'll have a couple. One in my name, one in Superintendent Masters'."

The custodian grinned. "Hope you get a good horse, Super."

It was while the man was recording the wager that Winter came through the swing doors accompanied by Dorothy Clay. Crome turned towards them.

"Good morning, Cecil, Dorothy."

"Director. You wanted to see me?"

Crome explained the purpose of his visit. The custodian took the opportunity to ask Clay if she would care to buy a sweep ticket.

"No, thank you. I don't bet."

"Hardly a bet, Doctor. Just a flutter. Doctor Winter will have a quid's worth."

"He will not. Don't ask him. He does not bet, either."

The custodian stared at her, open-mouthed. Masters, an interested onlooker, was not left long in doubt as to the reason for the uniformed man's surprise.

"Doesn't bet? Doctor Winter? I've known him have a bob on a horse a score of times. He'll bet on anything. You ask him."

"I will not ask him. And he's too busy for you to interfere."

At that moment, Crome turned to Masters. "I'm so sorry not to have introduced you immediately. A bad habit of scientists, I'm afraid—to forget the niceties and get down to the subject in hand." He looked at Clay. "Dorothy, Cecil, this is Superintendent Masters. Doctors Clay and Winter."

Masters disliked handshakes during investigations. He could never rid his mind of the unpleasant thought that he could be shaking hands with a monster. But there was no avoiding them this time, because the woman scientist made the first move despite his own obvious reticence. Clay's hand was pudgy and moist. That of Winter dry and shrivelled. Masters thought they represented a tactile summing up of the visible impression he gained of their two owners. He was reminded of the two little figures that pop in and out of their china house to let the world know whether the weather is to be wet or dry.

"Doctor Clay is just going across to the library for me," said Winter. "So if you two gentlemen would care to come to my office. . . ?"

Green had joined Toinquet in the Security chief's private office in the original house. This was to the left of the main front door. Behind it lay Toinquet's general office and beyond that the central registry in which all classified documents were deposited in safety cupboards with combination locks.

Green was sitting astride an upright chair of varnished wood with a green plastic seat. A rather crumpled Kensitas dangled from his lower lip. He was watching as Toinquet approved duty roster lists of custodians and guards. The lists were being pre-

sented by a diminutive middle-aged woman whom Toinquet
addressed as Alice throughout. She wore rimless spectacles and
had a bird-like, colourless face. Even her clothing—which
appeared to be a hand-knitted costume—was carried out in thrush
colours which, Green thought, would be fine on the feathered
variety, but not on the human ones. But her choice in colours in
no way seemed to detract from her businesslike air nor the efficiency and forthrightness with which she presented her material and
answered her boss's questions. After she left, through the com-
municating door to the general office, Green asked: "She your
Man Friday?"

"Alice? Indispensable old girl. Ex-WRAC. She took the staff
college course many moons ago. Just the administrative part of
it. Passed with flying colours."

"What's she doing here then? Why isn't she a brigadier or
something?"

"Retired. Never married. We asked her to come here. Positively
vetted women of her calibre are hard to come by in out-of-the-
way places like this. The job suits a spinster, and it's one she
knows how to do better than any of us. She types, does confidential filing—the lot."

"Lucky old toff, you! Got a light, by the way?"

Toinquet threw over a box of Swan.

"Ta! Mind if I keep them?"

Toinquet shrugged. "You always were a scrounging bastard,
Greeny."

"That's what I'm paid to be. Now I want to scrounge some
information. Lists of climbing members, those who go on the
week-end jaunts and so on."

"Oh, yes. By the way, don't spread it around that I keep these
lists. The members wouldn't like it."

"Invasion of privacy?"

"They'd call it that."

Green thought this was typical of Toinquet. He'd produce some
bit of *sub rosa* information to prove his efficiency, but he'd keep
it well hidden in order not to jeopardise his popularity. Green
mentally summed him up as a two-faced bastard.

"How much do you really know of their private lives, Widow?"

"The picture builds up."

"Of who sleeps with who?"

"We don't get much of that."

"How much, exactly?"

"A bit among the unmarried. We've a young chap called Newsom, for instance, who's attractive to the birds. I know he has his bit of fun—handed to him on a plate."

"By the birds?"

"We have quite a number of young women here with B.Sc. degrees. They're the lab juniors, if you like. . . ."

"I've got a hierarchy list," said Green. "There's nearly thirty thousand boffins employed by the state and government sponsored scientific agencies. Funny thing is that there are more Principal Scientific Officers than Senior Scientific Officers, and more of them than Higher Scientific Officers. Like a South American navy —more admirals than matelots."

"Then there are Scientific Officers and lastly Assistant Scientific Officers. It's these last I was mentioning just now. They're knowledgeable and trained well enough to take readings, keep research notes and so on without the more qualified people having to worry whether the jobs are done properly or not. And it's among these that you usually find the bedworthies. Some of 'em aren't bad-lookers, particularly when the choice is limited."

"But no scandals—marriage break-ups, divorces and so on?"

Toinquet shook his head. "You're barking up the wrong tree if you're looking for motives in that area, Greeny."

"Glad to hear it. Now what about those lists?"

Toinquet opened a desk drawer and took out a file. "I had Alice bring these in earlier. The three trips you're interested in are marked. Help yourself. You won't mind if I carry on with a bit of work while you browse?"

Green was pleased to be left in peace to do his scanning. Armed, as he was, with the bits of gossip which each of his colleagues had repeated the night before, he had some idea of what to look for.

He had been glancing through the various sheets for several

minutes when there was a knock at the door and Hill came in. Toinquet looked up. "My men at the gate tell me you've been out."

Hill wasn't sure from the tone employed whether this was a question asking where he'd been and what he'd done; an accusation of having left barracks without a pass; or simply a statement to show that Toinquet was very much on the ball and that nothing that went on in the Centre escaped his eagle eye.

Hill, however, was not prepared to be fazed by it, whichever it was. He put his hand in his pocket, took out a packet of Kensitas and threw them across to Green. "I went to get the DI some fags from the village shop."

Toinquet stared in amazement. "We sell fags here, in the mess."

"Only at the bar," growled Green. "And that isn't open at nine in the morning."

"Oh!" It seemed Toinquet was not wholly convinced by the account. Green, switched-on enough to hoist inboard any oddity, immediately began to wonder why the Security man should disbelieve a perfectly innocent explanation. Was it just the natural nosiness demanded by his job, or was Toinquet intent on keeping abreast of every move made by the Yard men for some more personal reason? The thought was filed away in Green's prodigious memory to be answered later.

"Grab some of these lists," the DI said to Hill. "We've some comparing to do."

"Right." Hill turned to Toinquet. "By the way, I've left the car outside here. Is that all right for a bit?"

"If you haven't blocked the entrance or pinched the Director's place."

The two detectives got down to a murmured comparison of the lists, with Hill acting as note-taker. The job took more than three-quarters of an hour. When they were finished, Green said: "Right, Widow. Questions when you're ready."

Toinquet put his pen down.

"First off," said Green, "the people who were present on all the three fatal occasions. Crombie. Who's he?"

79

"Junior staff. Biological Sciences. Group Eight. Unmarried. Mountaineer. Keen."

"Banes?"

"Pal of Crombie. Also unmarried. Chemist. Group Four. Not so keen, but a climber. Usually accompanies Crombie."

"Winter? He's Doctor Winter, I suppose?"

"That's right. Secretary of the club. Runs the show. He's a walker. Head of Group Six."

"Clay?"

"Dorothy Clay. Deputy leader of Group Six. She tags along after Winter. Looks after him like a baby in his office and thinks she has to do it outside, too."

"You mean she goes for him in a big way?" asked Hill.

Toinquet stroked his chin. "Well, now, what do I say to that? She's no oil painting and no chicken. She's a bit mannish herself and yet I'd have said her one aim in life was to find a chap mug enough to take her on. But she tries too hard, if you get me. So I reckon she's settled for second best until a better opportunity crops up. Winter's a decent old stick and lets her wet-nurse him, but he's a married man."

"OK," said Green. "So we've got her background. But this chap Winter. He's a married man, you say, but he seems to be away every week-end. That doesn't add up. Where does he live?"

"In quarters here. His wife's in Dorset."

"He never sees her?"

"Not that I know of."

"You're supposed to know everything."

"When he goes on leave. He gets six weeks a year."

"So, he either doesn't like his missus, or he does like Doctor Clay. Does she live in, too?"

"Yes."

"Do they ever bunk up together?"

"No."

"You're sure?"

"Of course I'm sure."

"How? Do you keep a watch on their rooms? How far apart are they?"

"Practically next door to each other."

"So you wouldn't know if either of them went in for a bit of night hiking, would you?"

"It's ... it's unthinkable," said Toinquet.

"Not if what you've told us about her is true. She's after a man—any man. You've said so. She's latched on to a grass widower in the next bedroom. To me that adds up to a bit of hoop-lah on occasions."

Toinquet grew very red in the face. "I know them," he said angrily.

"OK, mate, keep your shirt on," said Green blithely. "I'll take your word for it that human nature's different in Pottersby from anywhere else. So we'll push on to somebody else."

"Who?"

"A character called Bullock."

"What about him?"

"Is he still here? If so, who is he? What is he?"

"Long-haired type. Forty odd. Unmarried. Lives in. Got a bit of private money. Chief Statistician."

"He used to be a great week-ender at one time. He went on every trip except two for over a year. Then a few months ago he stopped and hasn't been since. I wonder why? Has he got a woman around?"

"Alec Bullock? He's got an E type and flashes around a bit. My guess is he's not a womaniser—I mean, he's forty, can afford to marry and hasn't—so if he fancies a bit on the side I reckon he goes further afield. Probably up to the smoke."

"You're suggesting he flits about a bit. This total stoppage of climbing seems to indicate he's got a steady alternative."

"Not a woman. Not Alec. He's never far away at week-ends. Boozing perhaps. That's more likely."

"You're sure? It looked at one time as though he was a pretty keen walker or climber."

"He was. Mountaineer. Dead keen."

"But you'd not noticed that he'd chucked it recently?"

"I'll confess I hadn't. I'd realised he wasn't going quite so often, of course, but ... look, Greeny, I haven't been through those lists for some time. Until this blew up, there wasn't any need."

"No? Well, you're the Security king. But a cut-off as sharp as that might mean something."

"I'll see what I can find out."

"Don't bother on our account. We're more interested in having a word with Crombie, Banes, Winter and Clay and the other characters who went along for the ride on one or other of the three occasions and probably witnessed the falls. Your lists don't show which were non-climbers and non-walkers."

Toinquet was getting irritable. It was fairly obvious to Hill that Green—in accordance with his previously announced intentions—was needling the Security man purposely. Hill couldn't decide quite why Green thought it was necessary, even if the two old colleagues had never got on well together. Toinquet's air of infallibility was irritating, but certainly not enough to give Green grounds for suspecting that Toinquet knew more about the tragedies than he was disclosing. If Green was right, thought Hill, it would be a pretty turn-up for the book because—as they had argued last night—knowledge of that description in a Security man could only mean implication; and implication in a crime such as this which, Hill was convinced, was most likely to be the work of only one man, would indicate sole guilt.

"That's easy enough," snapped Toinquet. "Here, hand me the lists. By now it should have occurred to you that usually the same number go each week because . . ."

"Because the coach is a thirty-two seater," said Green blithely, "and if they can fill all the seats it comes cheaper. But on nine occasions in the last thirteen and a half months they have had less than the maximum—dropping as low as twenty-seven in the middle of last January."

"The super-cargo on the days you are interested in is . . ." Toinquet turned the pages rapidly. "Silk's day . . . Doctor and Mrs Newmills. He's a bug-hunter and his wife's an artist, not employed at the Centre. She goes along to sketch sometimes. Then there was young Overton who's no longer with us. He's teaching somewhere. Miss Pewsey, Miss Horsely and Mrs Long-

worth. They're all junior scientists although Miss Pewsey is now
Mrs Lydney. Lydney himself is one of the Materials Research
Group. He's a physical metallurgist."

"That the lot?"

"No. Doctor and Mrs Roslin. He's a physicist. Lord knows
what she is. Runs the local Girl Guides, I believe."

"So she'd take to the great outdoors like a duck to water. What
about her husband?"

"Amateur photographer. He'd have spent the week-end trying
to get the best light and shade view of Ullswater, I suppose."

"Thanks. Any more? No? What about Redruth's day?"

"Miss Horsley and Mrs Longworth again. You'll see there isn't
a Mister Longworth. She's a divorcée of about thirty-eight. She
and Horsley go along for the laughs and do the cooking. Along
with them was Trott who's busy on energy release and heat
transfer at the moment—in the same group as Lydney. And that's
all. And then this last week-end there was an Applied Mathematician from the Engineering Group—Morrison. Higham, a physicist.
They're both fishermen actually. Swinton and Mrs Swinton. He's
Admin staff—straight civil servant. She's not employed here.
Sergeant Hill will probably have seen her if he went to the paper
shop in Pottersby. . . ."

"The fat, fair one, or the thin dark one?" asked Hill calmly,
not prepared to be caught out by this oblique question.

"She's darkish," admitted Toinquet. "She works mornings in
the shop. And that's the lot."

"Thanks. Got all those, Sergeant?"

"Every blessed one, sir. The kooloo."

"Good." Green got to his feet. "Thanks, Widow. I'll try not to
worry you again. It's going to take me and the sarn't here quite
a time seeing these people. . . ."

"What? All of them?"

"Why not? That's what we're here for."

"And the best of British! Let me know what you find out. I'll
be interested to know if you get anything I haven't got."

"Sure?" asked Green, choosing a cigarette carefully from the
new packet.

"Of course I'm sure. What the hell do you think I am? I want to know if I'm missing something, and I want anything you get for my files."

"Right, Widow, start writing. Doctor Alec Bullock stopped climbing because he had a dizzy spell on a mountain and the experience frightened him so much he decided to jack it in."

"Ah! Well at any rate I knew it wasn't on account of a woman."

Green paid no attention to the interruption. "And since then, he has amused himself at week-ends with Mrs Mailer, widow of the dead man."

"What? You're raving, Greeny. Mrs Mailer's a lush bit, but she's classy and particular."

"In that case, I wonder what Bullock was doing in her bed yesterday when she got the news that her husband had fallen off a mountain?"

"I don't believe it."

At least this time Green had no doubts that Toinquet was telling the truth. His well-shaved, florid face showed all the classic signs of incredulity, together with dismay. It caused Green to wonder even more about his former colleague. The incredulity he could understand. Toinquet had, over the years, obviously made his own assessment of each of the boffins in the Centre. He had mentally catalogued each as being of a certain type. With justification and, probably, a fair amount of success. To find certain of his flock acting out of the characters he had assigned to them could be cause for disbelief. To hear of this alleged stepping out of character from people who had arrived in the Centre less than twenty-four hours before could be a further cause for scepticism. All this Green could accept. In Toinquet's shoes he would have felt the same doubts. Would even have scoffed at the idea. But dismay! That was something different. Capable, Green knew of two interpretations. Dismay at having failed to realise that Bullock and Mrs Mailer were having an affair or—and this is what interested Green most—or perhaps dismay that the Yard team had discovered this fact. A fact that could prove inconvenient for Toinquet?

Swiftly, Green considered this. If the last point were true, it would have to mean that Toinquet was aware of the liaison, otherwise he could not be dismayed by its discovery. And, Green thought, Toinquet's surprise at the news had been genuine enough. So probably the dismay was only that occasioned by a large hole in his security net being pointed out to a man who prided himself inordinately on the completeness of his grasp of what went on in his preserve. Green sighed mentally at not being able to claim another nail for Toinquet's coffin.

Surprised by the momentary pause, Hill looked at Green who nodded to him, then turned to Toinquet. "As well as getting the DI some fags this morning, I called on Mrs Mailer."

"I still don't believe it. I'll go and ask Bullock now."

"Where will you find him?"

"In the Statistics Office, upstairs."

Green said slowly: "You're up to something, Widow. You knew Sarn't Hill had gone out. But you didn't know Bullock had. That means your guards don't normally report traffic at the gate to you as a routine. But they have been told to report our movements. Why? What's so interesting about our comings and goings?"

Toinquet tried bluster.

"Everybody who's not a regular employee at the Centre is reported."

"Direct to you? At the time? Wherever you are? Come off it, Widow. We're worrying you, matey. You're hiding something."

Nobody spoke after this. Toinquet was not even struggling for words in which to reply. The silence began to make Hill feel uncomfortable. At last Green struck a match for his unlit cigarette and flicked the dead stalk expertly at Toinquet's waste bin before sauntering out of the office.

Brant said: "I've been hanging about waiting for you."

Cynthia Dexter, wearing green slacks and a rust-red roll-neck sweater, with a white lab coat over her arm, smiled warmly. "I'm flattered. But you could have come to my room and knocked. Or don't policemen enter girls' bedrooms without warrants?"

"Invitation's enough. But what I wanted to talk about has

nothing to do with you as a prospective suspect, so I wouldn't treat you as one."

"That's sweet of you. By the way, as you were so gallant as to escort me to supper last night, can I return the compliment tonight and invite you to join me at The Bull in Pottersby for dinner?"

Brant grinned. "You certainly can, Doctor."

"Good. I'm walking across to my lab. Can we talk as we go?"

Brant fell in beside her. She said: "You were very prompt with your acceptance. No question of asking your Superintendent first. Does that mean you've been assigned to me for some reason? Or is your time always your own on murder enquiries?"

Brant reddened. "You're a sharp one, Doctor. Yes! I have been assigned to you."

"Again I'm flattered."

"For ten minutes only . . ."

"Now you're spoiling it."

"Just long enough to ask you if you've remembered anything more about that bet you thought Doctor Silk had made."

"Actually, I *have* been thinking about it."

"And?"

"I'm not usually undecided about things, but I don't know whether to be pleased or sorry I mentioned that bet."

"Why?"

"I should be pleased at the thought of helping you. But when I wondered why you were so interested last night, it hit me like a brick that the first thought that entered your head was that if you could find out who bet Stanley Silk he couldn't climb that face alone, you would have identified the murderer. Do you deny that?"

"What would be the use of denying anything to a woman with a mind like yours? As I said, you're sharp."

"I'm being serious, Sergeant Brant. I should hate to be the one to point the finger of suspicion at one of my colleagues."

"Me, too—in your place. But there have been three deaths— among those same colleagues. Don't you think it's time they stopped?"

"The climbing club is going into suspended animation. The committee took the decision last night. So the falls will stop."

"Will they? Falls from mountains, perhaps. But will the deaths stop? You don't have to have a mountain handy in order to kill somebody."

They walked on in silence for a few moments.

"You really think there could be others?"

"I don't want to frighten you. In fact, we can't yet say for certain that there have been any murders . . ."

"But you're convinced there have been three."

"Successful attempts, yes."

She stopped dead in her tracks and stared at him. "You mean there may have been others which didn't come off?"

"There are . . . shall we say, indications."

"Oh, god!" She started to walk again slowly.

"The truth is," said Brant quietly, "that these things feed on themselves. Somebody thinks he's got away with it. That makes him cocky. He thinks he can get away with it again and again and again. And after three successful tries he probably thinks . . ."

"Please stop! I recognise the truth of what you're saying, and your ten minutes are nearly up."

Brant took her by the arm and turned her to face him. She had tears in her eyes. He spoke gently. "The mention of ten minutes was merely to assure you I wasn't going to tail you, keep an eye on you and generally make a nuisance of myself. It didn't mean that I think I'm such a bloody good interrogator or so attractive personally that I can get any good-looking woman to give me anything I want inside ten minutes."

"No?"

His voice gruffened. "Hell! We're back thinking about the student's-eye view of the fuzz."

She gave a thin wisp of a smile. Just enough to tremble her lips. "You're not a very good detective, after all."

"And just what do you mean by that?"

She began to walk again, in silence.

"I asked you a question."

87

"And I'm wondering whether to answer it, or just to keep my big mouth shut."

Brant, walking beside her but looking straight ahead, replied: "It's not nine o'clock in the morning yet. Hardly the time of day to say to a girl that she hasn't got a big mouth to keep shut and to add that when she does open it she looks so kissable it just isn't true. But I'm saying it now."

She made no reply.

He looked down at her. "Well, what have you got to say to that?"

She smiled up at him, her lips pursed exaggeratedly. After a moment she said: "I said nothing because I couldn't be seen being kissed by a policeman in broad daylight in the middle of the Centre for all to see."

Brant blushed and grinned sheepishly. "Don't give me ideas."

"I thought you already had them." She took his arm. "I do want to help you, and I see the force of your argument. I racked my brain last night."

"And?"

"I'm fairly sure it was Cecil Winter who had that bet with Stanley Silk."

"Thank you."

"But I'm as sure as I can be that Cecil would not try to kill Stanley."

"In that case, I can assure you he will have nothing to fear from us."

Brant was conscious that, as he used these words—sincere as he was—they sounded trite even to him. He noted with some pleasure, however, that Cynthia appeared to accept them at their face value, although he would have been prepared to swear that such would not have been the case twelve hours earlier.

Masters was surprised by the neatness and pleasant aspect of Winter's office. It was about as big as the study bedroom which had been allotted to him. An electric fire added to the warmth of the central heating, but that wasn't what provided the welcoming air. The glass top of the desk shone, the woodwork gleamed cosily; print curtains at the window gave a splash of colour and two vases of daffodils brought the living sunshine in. This was no man's room—there was a woman's touch here.

Winter, scrawny and brown, was wearing grey trousers and an old sports jacket. The pockets bulged with whatever it was he carried on his person. His lab coat, clean for the new week and heavily starched, hung on a coat-hanger on a chromium stand.

As the group leader took his seat behind the desk, Masters noticed that the claw-like nails, which continued the contours of the long, loose-skinned fingers, were dotted with chalky deposits, and wondered as to the cause. Incipient rheumatism or arthritis? Or just senility heralding its approach?

The voice was high-pitched. "You're a curious man, Mr Masters. I suppose you could go out of here and write a complete inventory of this office."

Masters was flicked on the raw by the tone and the content of the accusation. Chiefly because it was said without humour, but additionally because in the first place he'd merely been admiring the room and, furthermore, he disliked the insinuation that he was so lacking in good manners as to be more inquisitive in such matters than good manners normally allow.

"I doubt it. I was wondering how the Centre managed to find such gems among cleaning staff—ones that would polish and garnish with flowers. . . ." As he said this, the thought struck him that cleaners in the Centre would need to be vetted and supervised pretty closely. The innumerable facets of security in such a place must be a headache for Toinquet.

"We rely entirely on retired service men," said Crome. "They're amazingly good. Of course, they're not badly off, in that they're already in receipt of service pensions, then they have their pay here which, thank heaven, is supplemented appreciably by the X factor which is compounded not only of unsocial hours payments, but also of danger money. There is, of course, little risk here, but you know what bureaucracy and trades unionism is. Cleaners at Porton, who may catch a bug, get it, so everybody everywhere in the same grade gets it. I believe we have quite an army of them —certainly more than twenty."

"Lucky you! Flowers in rooms . . ."

Winter coughed. "Excuse me, but the flowers are by courtesy of my deputy, Doctor Clay. She shares this office and tends to pamper me in the process of pandering to her own tastes."

Masters nodded understandingly. "I thought there was a woman's touch about it." At the same time he wondered about the juxtaposition of White Devil words like pamper and pander. Was Winter a precise man when it came to words? Did he, subconsciously, intend to convey that Doctor Clay over-indulged him as a means of gratifying her own clandestine amours?

"What were you anxious to question me about, Director?" asked Winter, virtually ignoring Masters.

Crome turned to the Yard man. "The ball is in your court, Superintendent."

"Thank you. Doctor Winter, I realise my visit to the Centre may be distasteful to you and, indeed, to everybody here. Nobody likes policemen on the premises, particularly when they are investigating the cause of the deaths of colleagues and all that that implies. However, I should be grateful for whatever co-operation you can afford me, so that my stay here can be cut to the minimum."

"Success being the key to your length of stay?"

"I hope so. Though I should like you to believe me when I say I would rather uncover a mare's nest than a murderer."

"If you say so. But I can't believe feathers for caps are so easily come by that you would gladly forego one."

"Cecil, please!" said Crome.

"I rejoice in my feathers as much as any brave," said Masters urbanely. "Can you please tell me whether, within your working brief, there are any alternative lines of investigation?"

"I don't understand that question."

Masters mentally cursed Winter. The last thing he wanted was to become involved in a high-powered scientific discussion because he would then be at a loss. But it seemed as if the leader of Group Six was not prepared to fight anywhere but on his own ground.

"As I understand it, Doctor, the scientists in this group under your leadership are researching ways and means of shielding tactical nuclear reactors. Without wishing to know any of the details of your work, I wondered if you could tell me whether there are several theories as to how this may ultimately be achieved."

"Of course there are," snapped Winter. "The Director does not blinker us. And if there were only one way, there would be no need for researching the project. We would have the answer at our fingertips."

"In that case, would you mind telling me whether each of your colleagues regards the various alternatives as tenable, or are there separate schools of thought among you, each school devoted strongly to its own theory?"

Winter didn't answer. Crome turned to Masters. "There's a directness about you that even I find frightening."

"Why, sir? Have I put my finger on a sore point?"

"No, you haven't," said Winter adamantly. "But you are attempting to stir up dissension."

"In what way, Doctor? I have asked a question. If you are not prepared to answer it . . ."

"I know that one. You will draw your own conclusions." Winter turned to Crome. "I must ask you, Director, if, during your conversation with the Superintendent, you have indicated to him that there is a slight clash of opinion within the group on our varying approaches to the current objective?"

"Cecil," said Crome, "you know me better than that. I consider it my duty to help Mr Masters as much as lies within my power, but that does not include pin-pointing areas of professional dissension or suggesting that differences of approach in a laboratory are carried over into life outside. Three men have died. In suspicious circumstances. Mr Masters knows that such deaths are usually the result of hatred, envy or jealousy. As all these men were employed within this group, he naturally looks within the group for signs of these emotions. I don't have to prompt him. He knows his job."

"You are here with him."

"For various reasons. The first, obviously, because the final responsibility for whatever goes on in the Centre is mine. I also feel that my presence at interviews such as this is a protection for my colleagues as well as a help to the police."

"Very well." Winter turned to Masters. "There *are* various differences of opinion here. Our main effort has been concentrated on determining whether deuterium oxide has the necessary density in practical amounts to provide the protection needed. However, there are other suggestions. For instance, one point of view, based on the simple principle of the inverse square law . . ."

"Double the distance, quarter the force? Treble the distance, one-ninth of the force?" asked Masters.

Crome chuckled. Winter scowled.

"Using this principle, it has been postulated there is a possibility of capturing slowed-down particles by means of a magnetic field. To condense them, in fact, to produce energy. I won't go into the technical details of the Pinch Theory . . ."

"I think I can envisage—as a layman—what you are suggesting," said Masters. "Would I be right in saying that as the particles have mass they are therefore subject to the normal laws of gravity and so could be attracted by a magnetic field?"

This time Crome laughed. "As you so rightly disclaimed—a layman's view. But it comes close. The normal laws of gravity as you call them—as Newton expounded them—unfortunately do not apply in their entirety in the field of particle physics. If they did, our problem might be easier. We could collect the particles like iron filings on a schoolboy's magnet. But, within reason, you're close."

Even Winter thawed a little. "I won't bother you with talk of laser beams for fusing, plasma, spherical magnetic fields round voids, magnetic bottles and so on. Suffice it to say there is a theory, with sub-theories, based on this approach."

"Any others?" asked Masters, slightly gratified to find Winter yielding and anxious to make the most of this moment.

"Oh, yes." There was a little pause before Winter continued. "There's what I call the ultra-violet school. As you appear to have some grasp of physics, you will not be unaware that the earth is daily bombarded with just those particles and rays we are seeking to contain. Fortunately for us, the atmosphere stops the dangerous ultra-violet light from scorching us up. Quite simply, the thought is that if the atmosphere can create a barrier to stop the emanations from the source of all the world's energy, namely the sun, why should not we be able to recreate an atmosphere in miniature to serve the same purpose *vis-à-vis* the emanations from a small reactor."

"Are those the sum of the theories, Doctor Winter?"

"How many do you suppose one small unit can sustain?"

"May I ask which theory you favour personally?"

Winter said drily: "I thought I'd already told you that our major effort has been concentrated on the deuterium oxide project."

"So you did. But the others have your blessing?"

"In my small way, Superintendent, I must needs be a diplomat. Whilst ensuring that the energy of my group is not wantonly dissipated in hare-brained schemes, I must offer support, when needed, to alternative approaches which I personally may not view with particular favour.'

"I understand, Doctor. I think that disposes of the professional questions I wish to ask you for the moment."

"Surely there is the final one?"

"You mean I should ask you which of your colleagues supports which theory?"

"That would seem to be the object of the questioning so far."

"Would you be prepared to tell me?"

"No. But I hoped you would have asked."

"Doctor Winter, whenever possible I try to avoid getting egg on my face—unnecessarily, that is."

"Cecil," said Crome, "there's a shrewdness here as great as any we may pride ourselves in possessing in the Centre. Can we please get on with the business in hand?"

Winter spread his thin hands. "I am here. Director."

Masters stepped in quickly. "You must have expected me to ask you some questions about the climbing and walking club. This time I won't disappoint you."

"Very well. What do you wish to know?"

"When I first heard of it, I was a little surprised that you should have a flourishing club of about two hundred members."

"It is gratifying, but don't be misled by numbers. By far the greater proportion is made up of walkers and these, in their turn, vary between the genuine fell and hill enthusiasts and the fine afternoon strollers."

"I appreciate that. Yet you manage to take a coach-load off every week-end summer and winter alike."

"Except for a week or two around Christmastime, yes."

"That argues enthusiasm."

"Does it? About twelve and a half per cent of the club at any one time? We fill those coaches up regularly with non-members who go along for the ride."

"If you are disappointed in the turn-outs, why not cut the number of trips?"

"Economics."

"We get the coach very cheaply because we book it for every week-end. Unit cost would soon soar were we to cut the number of hirings."

"Economics are that important?"

"Did you ever encounter an organisation where they weren't?"

"No. But there is a question of degree."

"To be sure. As a profession, government scientists are not well paid. Many of us, in places like this, are faced with frequent moves, temporary hirings and so on. All come expensive. Also, climbing gear is expensive. It has been my aim here to popularise the sport and to make it as inexpensive as possible. To this end we have attempted to supply all the necessary gear—other than personal clothing—that we can." He looked at Masters as though expecting some reaction. Masters could not resist the urge to show that his own thought processes were no less nimble than his.

"Very wise. I assume that you have bought, say, two dozen sets of equipment. These should suffice for the greatest number that ever goes climbing at any one time and it saves sixty or seventy mountaineers from buying and maintaining gear."

Winter smiled frostily. "You've even got the number of sets right. It is indeed two dozen. Now, how have we managed this?"

Crome looked across at Masters expressively. Winter now had

94

the bit between his teeth and on this favourite topic it appeared he would be as verbose as formerly he had been taciturn. Masters guessed Crome would like to cut the flow short, but he, Masters, was prepared to listen all day if necessary—for the simple reason that the more people talked, the more they gave away.

"You mean, how have you managed to afford the gear?"

"Yes. The Centre was, initially, given the usual meagre grant for social and welfare purposes that all government domiciliary institutions are afforded at their inception. How far do you imagine a mere three hundred and fifty pounds would go in providing such items as a piano, billiards table, television set and the like—to say nothing of maintaining them, once bought?"

"It wouldn't scratch the surface."

"Quite right. We managed a television and a table-tennis table, I believe, did we not, Director?"

Crome nodded.

"Of course," went on Winter, "we have a mess contribution and there are bar profits. Out of these, the Director has very kindly alloted us small sums, as indeed he has to all the clubs and societies in the Centre. This has enabled us, by clever buying, to equip ourselves with light-weight frames, rucksacks, a tent or two and so forth. Some of it has come from government surplus sales at very low prices, the rest from ordinary trade outlets. The result has been that our club membership fee has been kept down to the very modest sum of two pounds fifty a year—a great consideration in maintaining and increasing membership."

Winter was obviously expecting surprised congratulations for management ability. Masters, seeking for some remark not too banal, said: "You're doing a marvellous job, Doctor Winter, and I notice that you've been very modest in not mentioning the fact that if the club owns the equipment, somebody—presumably you —has the unenviable task of maintaining it, issuing it, collecting it in, chasing up forgetful members and so on."

"You see a problem in its entirety," said Winter. "I like that. But you were mistaken when you presumed that I acted as the club's quartermaster. Doctor Clay does that for us. The Director

95

has very kindly allowed us to use a small storeroom in this building." He got to his feet. "You must see how extremely well Doctor Clay looks after our assets. Just along the passage from here."

He opened the door and led the way. Inside a dozen paces he reached a solid, green door and switched on the light inside. The little room was, in fact, a dark room, with slatted shelving round the walls. Here the climbing equipment had been laid out in sets, each piece numbered in white paint. Rucksack number three was ranged with light-weight carrier three, water-bottle three, even enamel mug number three.

"There you are," said Winter. "A place for everything, and everything in its place. When you consider that many of these sets were in use over the week-end, you will appreciate how admirable is Doctor Clay's work on our behalf."

"All back, apparently, except set number six," said Masters, gazing at an empty space on the shelf.

Winter's tone dropped. "I imagine that was the set being used by poor Mailer. We shall probably get it back when the police and hospital authorities return his effects."

They left the little room. In the corridor outside, Masters said to Winter: "Thank you very much, Doctor. I don't think I need take up any more of your time at the moment. I hope I shall see you again in the mess, perhaps."

Winter lived up to his reputation of being 'a nice old stick' sufficiently to smile toothily and to wish Masters luck.

As Crome and Masters left the complex, the Superintendent was assessing the recent interview and, more importantly, Winter's attitude. Crome seemed to appreciate this and remained silent.

Nowhere in the conversation had Winter given Masters any hint that the Group Six building held any secrets other than those directly connected with the work carried on there. Winter's attitude—a bit anti at first—could be accepted for what it appeared to be on the surface. Any man who has had three of his colleagues killed is going to be a little suspicious of everybody thereafter—including the investigating police. Nerves, being what they are, sometimes cause even the best-tempered and co-operative of men to appear hostile until soothed by diplomacy. Winter had thawed

eventually, presumably when he realised that Masters was prepared to conduct his enquiries in a fairly civilised manner, without notebooks, cautions, diverse interrogation techniques and all
the other hoorah methods so often credited to the police.

"Got it all sussed out? I believe that's the phrase, isn't it?"
asked Crome after a while. Masters noted that the Director
seemed somewhat happier than earlier on. Their time together
seemed to have served to put him more at his ease: to cause him
to adopt a slightly jocular tone. Was he, too, relieved to discover
that police methods were not necessarily compounded of ringing
bells, flashing lights and recorded interviews? Or, and Masters
felt a pang of guilt about this, had he himself somehow given
Crome a wrong impression concerning the conduct of this case?
Had anything he had said led the Director to believe that the
investigation would not be pressed home to the full? If so, Crome
would have another shock coming to him. Of course, there was
just the possibility that the Director, having seen and heard how
Masters worked, was now convinced that he was a match—and
more than a match—for the Yard team; presupposing Crome was
the guilty party.

"I have nothing sussed out, Director. It's early days yet. When I
fish in a pond the size of this, not being familiar with the water, I
usually take a little time to decide which ground bait to use—or
hooks, or flies, or weight of line, or whether I need a huge drag-
net to land my prey. But whichever it is, I try to go about it fairly
quietly and gently. There's little point in stirring up the sludge
on the bottom to muddy the water so that nobody—not even the
fish—can see what they're doing."

"Do I detect a warning tone in your description of what I
consider to be a gratifying way of conducting your enquiry?"

"I think perhaps that is what I intended, Director, because there
is one measure which I am prepared to take to land my fish—
should it become necessary—which I didn't mention."

"I believe I know what you're going to say."

"You do?"

"You would drain the pond to pick him up—if all else failed."
Masters looked across at him as they walked.

"I would try to filter through to safety the small fry and the innocents."

"I'm sure. I am extremely grateful that you haven't started draining operations already."

"Draining is hard work. A murder HQ set up; hundreds of interrogations and written reports; scores of files and hundreds of cross-checks; phones brought and clerks doing shift-work on a rota basis, conferences every few hours . . . you can imagine it, I daresay. It is a very useful way of going about things on occasions, but here it would be terribly disruptive. I would prefer to spare you and myself that experience. Watching the water and casting the right line in the right place is the method I usually use."

"Some fish—even those whose identity is known—often refuse bait, I understand. I have heard tell of big 'uns that have stead-fastly refused, for years, to be hooked."

"That is, I believe, a notable characteristic of the pike," said Masters drily. "And to translate it into human terms, a pike or piker is a gambler—one who dices with danger. I would never put my money on the punter—always on the bookie."

"Still that element of warning," said Crome, frowning slightly. "I wonder why? I pay you the compliment of supposing it to be intentional."

Masters felt happier. He felt he had really got through to Crome; conveyed to him his firm intention of seeing the case through to the bitter end.

"Thank you. It was intentional."

"For any particular reason? Was in personal, for instance?"

"Strictly speaking it was a general warning that this business may be long, hard and upsetting to the Centre as a whole. But I feel you must accept it as a personal warning, too."

"May I ask why?"

"Because murder enquiries are like wars. Nobody wins. Nobody comes out unscarred. You have more to lose than anybody—except, possibly, the murderer. I hate to think of anybody paying a penalty he has not incurred—or should I say a higher penalty than he has incurred?"

"Meaning that whatever the outcome of this, I am in some way to blame?"

"It may turn out that way. It may have been as a direct result of some decision of yours, as Director, that certain personalities were hired, fired, thrown together, separated or given certain tasks, any of which could have laid the groundwork for the present situation."

"Agreed. But I would have liked to hear you include the word 'unwitting' to describe any action of mine which may have precipitated such events."

"I would do that willingly, Director, but I feel I should point out that you are not paid to be unwitting."

"Nor am I. But am I to understand that you seriously suggest that ignorance is no defence?"

"I would sound more charitable, Director, if enquiries had been put in hand after the second death. It would not have lessened the crime, but it might have saved Mailer."

Crome's hand was on his forehead. "You're an unnerving man, Superintendent. We are speaking now from hindsight, but I cannot for the life of me think of one good reason why I should not have asked for enquiries to be made after Redruth's death. *Mea culpa*! I am the Director here, and as such . . ." He spread his hands. "Somewhere along the line you reckon I shall get it in the neck for so obvious an oversight! And the penalty may be greater than that which my sin of omission may have incurred! Thank you, Superintendent, for the elucidation. Do you know, I have had this in the back of my mind all along—the probable penalty, not the sin. And yet I feel it has done me good to realise that you thought this through so clearly. I feel it is a sort of insurance—your understanding will protect me and all of us here from some gross miscarriage of justice."

"Did you fear that, too?"

"I confess it. At first. Mistakes are so easy to make, so difficult to rectify."

Chapter 5

MASTERS PARTED FROM Crome outside the front door of the old house. He had seen Brant lurking, at a discreet distance, as he and the Director had walked back from the Group Six laboratory. Now he turned in the direction of the Sergeant, who hurried towards him.

"Something to tell me, Brant?"

"Yes, Chief. Miss Dexter remembered who made that bet with Silk."

Brant seemed slightly uneasy in the telling, and Masters had a momentary pang of remorse at using the growing friendship between Brant and Cynthia for such purposes. It was this feeling that dictated his next question.

"She told you willingly?"

Brant reddened. "No, Chief. But she told me."

"Who was it?"

"Winter."

"Let's get it straight, Sergeant. Miss Dexter told you that Winter bet Silk that he, Silk, couldn't get up a particular climb alone?"

"It was a race for a bottle of whisky, Chief. Winter was to walk up, Silk was to climb. Whoever got to the top first won."

"I see. That marches."

"Beg your pardon, Chief?"

"Nothing. Just thinking aloud. What's the matter with you, Sergeant? You look a bit pained about something? Was Miss Dexter difficult?"

"Not exactly, Chief. She didn't like it, of course."

"And?"

"Well, Chief, she wants me to go out to dinner with her tonight."

Masters realised that the news pleased him. Obviously no irreparable harm had been done to the relationship between the sergeant and his lady scientist.

"I don't see why that should upset you."

"You mean it's all right for me to go?"

Masters looked straight at Brant. "Sergeant, you're a grown man . . ."

"But the case, Chief!"

Masters felt for his tobacco tin. "The unwelcome and tiresome duty of accompanying Miss Dexter to dinner is in the furtherance of our investigation, which means you may use the car. I'm awfully sorry you've had this rather dull chore thrust on you, Brant, but there you are! And please remember, as I said, you are a grown man, and within reason, you do as you like. The only limitation on whatever action you take—ever—is that you need to be in a position to give a good reason for taking it if asked for one later."

"Thanks, Chief."

"Is she personable, your Miss Dexter?"

"I think you'd find her . . . yes, Chief, she's great."

"Good. I'd like to meet her some time. Where are the DI and Hill?"

"I saw Hill a few minutes ago. He said they'd sorted out a list of climbing club members as long as your arm and were interviewing them one by one."

"In that case, I'll leave them to it. There's a library in the house. I'm going in there."

"What about me, Chief?"

"See if you can help the DI."

As he and Crome had not encountered Doctor Clay on the way back from Group Six, Masters was hoping she would still be in the library. If she were, it might be a convenient time and place for having a chat with her. He asked the guard in the hall for the library and was directed upstairs to the northern wing, where a number of former bedrooms had been converted into a library. He entered the one marked Technical, and saw it was deserted except for a woman sitting behind a desk in what had been a dressing room.

"Doctor Clay was here earlier. Have you tried Reference and Non-Technical?"

"Not yet."

"They're all in this wing."

"Hasn't the house got a library proper? Old houses of this size usually had large rooms. . . ."

"There is one. On the ground floor. It is now the computer room. Air-conditioned and all that." The librarian sounded slightly cross that a machine should merit such comfort while she was relegated to makeshift quarters.

"I see. Thank you."

He tried Reference and lastly, Non-Technical, without seeing Dorothy Clay. In this last room he found what was virtually a lending library for private reading: novels, autobiographies, rose-growing, history, motor-car racing, small-boat sailing, climbing, mountaineering . . .

He picked out a book on this last subject and opened it at random.

'Where the party is large,' he read, 'each member's personal gear should be individually marked, particularly items like cutlery, mugs and water-bottles. These should be used only by the owner: it is difficult to wash them really clean in camp conditions and if used communally they can serve to pass germs among the party, causing stomach upsets.'

He turned over a few more pages and read:

'THE CLIMBING SEQUENCE:

'There should always be at least sixty feet of rope between each two climbers, and the leader will need much more on most routes. . . .'

That, he thought, seemed to be in keeping with what Tom Hawker was reported to have said concerning the amount of rope Redruth had paid out before leaving his novice companion on the first ledge, and obviously the society was following the precepts of the experts in the way they allocated stores. He put the book back and wandered out on to the landing. A red cross on a white board, with an arrow pointing further along the corridor and the words MEDICAL TREATMENT CENTRE, made him wonder whether he should look in on Partington. But the thought that the post-mortem report on Mailer could not yet be through caused him to go downstairs and outside again. He had reached the tarmac when a two-fingered whistle cut through the air. He looked up and saw Green some distance away down one of the narrow paths which led to the laboratories. Green was lumbering towards him. As Masters looked up, the DI waved a beckoning arm.

"Struck oil?" asked Masters as Green came up.

"Maybe." Despite his laconic reply, there was an air of satisfaction—almost one of suppressed excitement—about Green. "I've just been talking to a chap called Doctor Roslin. He's a physicist, but he's also an amateur photographer. He and his wife went along with the bus that went to the Lake District."

"When Silk died?"

"That's right. I . . . don't look round, but we're being watched."

"Who by?"

"Widow Twankey—who else? Out of his office window. He's standing far back, but he's getting an eyefull."

Masters relit his dead pipe deliberately. "Perhaps that's one of his usual observation posts. I don't doubt he's always taking furtive peeps at somebody."

"Us, mostly, this morning," replied Green. He's keeping close tabs on us, an' trying to catch us out. Me, I reckon he's hiding something from us and watching to see we don't discover what it is."

Masters started to move away from the house. "You'd better tell me about it."

Green, falling in beside him, recounted very carefully his earlier meeting with Toinquet. How the security man had ordered his guards to report the Yard team's movements. How he had tried to catch Hill out over the assistants he saw in the tobacconist's shop.

"And now he's been watching us," said Masters. "What do you make of it?"

"As I said, for my money, he's hiding something from us. Or hoping to. And as we're here to look into multiple murder . . . well, why try to hide something we're not looking for?"

Masters walked on in silence for a moment. Then—

"You are suggesting he should go higher on the suspect list?"

"At the top of it."

"If he's keeping such a watchful eye on us, it will be difficult to start investigating him without him getting to know."

"Or it might flush him out."

"Of course. That was your plan from the beginning, wasn't it? But I wonder . . ."

"You don't think I'm right to try an' panic him," accused Green.

"What? Oh, yes, I agree with you. I was wondering what Toinquet could hope to achieve by keeping us under observation. After all, when we arrived last night he seemed not to have anything on his mind. What's caused him to change? Could it be your threat to keep an eye on him?"

Green scratched an ear and then wiggled a forefinger inside it as if to clear it of wax. It irritated Masters who, though aware that such anti-social gestures were usually a sign that Green was thinking deeply, nevertheless preferred to observe the graces of behaviour.

"I reckon," pronounced Green at last, "that he's been knocked off his perch by our form of investigation. What Widow was expecting was a crowd of fingerprint boys and photographers who'd concentrate on the job in hand and not pay any attention to anything outside it. When he realised we don't work that way, but pry into every hole an' corner, he began to get windy."

"What of?"

"Now you're asking. But I still reckon he knows something."

"In that case we'd better start looking at him in earnest. Can I leave it to you, as you seem to be the one he fears most."

"I'm game. I'll have a word with some of his guards a bit later. Now, what I came to see you about . . ."

"Doctor Roslin?"

"The same. He's an amateur photographer. He tells me he's got a movie shot of Silk climbing that mountain."

"Of the moment he fell?"

"Come off it," said Green. "You want jam on it."

"There's no harm in hoping. And if the sequence is just one of Silk climbing, it's not going to be much use to us."

"I've sent Brant to Roslin's house in the village to collect it. Roslin will show it to us. He's got a projector in his lab."

Green's tone clearly indicated to Masters that the DI had expected more enthusiasm to be shown over his discovery. If that was what he expected, thought Masters, he wasn't going to get it.

"Has he shown it to anybody else?"

"I asked him that. He said not. In fact, he was going to destroy it after Silk's death but never got round to it. Apparently not even his wife saw it. He just ran it through once when the reel came back and then put it aside. Said he'd forgotten all about it until I started asking questions."

They walked on, Green leading the way to another of the laboratory complexes, a replica of the one in which Group Six was housed. As they went, Masters told Green how Brant had learned that it was Winter who had laid the bet with Silk.

"So it's getting nearer home," grunted Green. "Three men killed. At least one of them trying to win a bet with his boss. Where does that leave Winter?"

"Definitely in the mind's eye."

"I'll say. And somebody knows it. That Clay dame, trying to prove to the custodian that Winter isn't a betting man!"

"I must admit I find that very interesting."

"Me, too. So, with Winter and Widow Twankey on our books, we can begin to build up a short list. In here." Green waved a rejecting hand to the custodian who made as if to stop him and carried on. "Roslin's office is down the left-hand corridor. He's the boss of this lot."

Roslin was a small man, bespectacled and bald. His white lab coat had been shortened to fit him, but the side pockets had not been lifted, so they hung, not just below his hips, but rather just above his knees. As it appeared he made full use of them for carrying bulky objects, the effect was ludicrous—or it might have been had the man himself not had an air of unconscious dignity which caught the attention and held it.

"You will understand," he said, "that I am an amateur photographer in the lowliest sense of the word. What I mean is, I make no pretence of emulating professional ability."

His voice was charming. As he explained himself, he was lowering the blinds in his office. As he moved to the projector on his desk he went on: "Perhaps you find that surprising."

"A little," murmured Masters. "Most enthusiasts strive for perfection in their hobbies."

"Ah, yes! I thought you would take that point of view. I needed a hobby that would be a relaxation. One which I could enjoy indulging, which might pay dividends, but which would make no demands on my time or my mind." He looked across at Masters and his eyes twinkled behind his spectacles. "I am, basically, an idle man. To do anything, to achieve anything, I have to drive myself, and I find the process more wearying than, I imagine, do most of my colleagues. That is why I take reels of film but never edit them. Most people view critically, cut and splice into pictorial accounts of holidays or journeys. I don't. I get great pleasure out of not doing it. And I get great pleasure simply from viewing everything I have filmed—warts an' all."

Roslin reached up to pull down the rolled screen. "You must understand that what I shall show you is not poor Silk's fall itself. I stopped filming when I saw he was in some distress. . . ."

"You mean," asked Green, "that you had the camera on him until you realised he was in difficulties and then lowered it?"

"Yes. I suppose I had some wild idea of being able to help in some way, or it was merely a reflex action caused by my unconscious desire to concentrate on what I subconsciously foresaw as drama. A professional with such precognition would, no doubt, have captured the fall on film. But, as I told you, I am the veriest of amateurs."

Amateur he may have been, but behind the dilettante approach there was still a first-class brain—one which automatically knew when and from where to take pictures. They had to wait for nearly three minutes of the reel to go before Silk appeared, but the subjects chosen and the composition of each sequence were a joy to Masters. Secretly he began to think that far from being too idle to edit his films, Roslin probably thought that not a single frame filmed by him should be discarded.

"Here he comes."

Silk hitching on his rope. Silk drinking from his water-bottle before setting out. Zoom lens showing handholds—push hold, jughandle, fingers clenched on a small hold, toe-jamming, foot and knee-jamming, wide bridging with Silk astride two downward clefts, Silk on a steep slab . . .

Silk cornering.

Then it was over. The continuation piece of film slapped through the threadway before Roslin could get back to it.

"I thought you said he was in distress," said Green.

"It isn't very apparent on so small a film. Perhaps if I were to move the projector back . . ."

On the second run-through it was just obvious that Silk was in physical difficulties. He was hanging on. The sideways shaking of the head was just discernible; then his head, which throughout the climb had been held high, had dropped between his outstretched arms.

"He was bushed," said Green.

"No," said Roslin firmly. "He was a fit man and an experienced climber. I know little of the craft, but I know from my own observation that there was nothing on that climb which could have challenged Silk's power or expertise."

Masters switched on the light.

"Thank you, Doctor Roslin. You have helped me more than I can say."

"How?" demanded Green.

"Have I really?" beamed Roslin. "I'm delighted. I have a great deal of faith in you policemen, and I must admit to being concerned about the untimely deaths of so many of my colleagues. Being present when Silk fell was an unnerving experience."

"Would you mind letting me have the film? I will, of course, return it."

"Of course you shall have it." Roslin busied himself putting the film into its yellow plastic cover. "There you are, Superintendent. Shall I seal and sign it?"

Masters smiled. "Sign it by all means, Doctor, but don't seal. I shall want to exhibit it."

"And you can't tell me why?"

"I'm sorry. It would be unethical to do so."

"In that case . . ." The little Doctor shook hands and showed them to the main door.

"I don't get it," growled Green. "What d'you want to lead the little chap on for? There was nothing in his magic lantern show to help us."

They were walking back towards the house. The day had cleared to a bright coldness which hardened outlines and cheered the setting appreciably.

"No leg-pull. I didn't have time to tell you earlier, but when I visited Winter, he proudly showed me the climbing club's store. They have a couple of dozen sets of climbing equipment. It was all there except set number six."

"And that's the set Mailer was using, I suppose. It will be at the hospital with his personal effects."

"Right. What set was Silk using in this film?"

"Christ! Don't tell me it was six?"

"It was. The zoom lens picked up the number on some of the items. Each number is writ large in white paint."

Green sucked a tooth. "Bit of a coincidence, eh?"

"Or an illuminated signpost."

They walked on in silence for a moment. Green broke it by saying: "So I suppose we're now going to see Bullock?"

"It's the obvious thing to do. Unless we can unearth some witness who can remember what the number of Redruth's set was."

"OK," said Green. "Say Bullock had set number six. Where does it get us?"

"I don't know. But I'm not prepared meekly to accept open-ended coincidences. Are you?"

"Am I hellers-like! And this makes Winter look even more like the man with the chopper."

"You've decided Toinquet isn't a candidate?"

"I'm not forgetting him. He tried to baffle me with a load of old bull this morning, and I don't like characters who keep a watchful eye on me."

"I can still leave Toinquet to you, then?"

"It'll be a pleasure." Green stopped suddenly in his tracks. "You know what I've forgotten? Widow Twankey probably has keys to every door in this laager. Or a master key. He's the one chap who could come and go anywhere at any time."

"Without being questioned," added Masters. "It's a useful thought."

Green grunted. "I'll ask around, just to make sure he's got a pass-key. And when I tackle him I'll make it sound so blasted significant he'll feel the cuffs on his wrists as I'm doing it."

"Crome, too, might have a pass-key. Look into that, too, while you're at it."

"The more the merrier. I'm beginning to feel happier about this job. It has possibilities. Pity old Winter won't have a key to his particular wigwam, otherwise I could have given him the shakes, too."

Masters felt he was at a loose end after Green had left him. Everybody at the Centre seemed to be busy. To talk to any one of them he would have first to decide whom he wished to interview and then seek that person out. His difficulty was to decide. Doctor Clay? Alec Bullock? Winter again? Mailer's immediate colleagues in Group Six?

He stayed in the open air, strolling, thinking, and smoking a full bowl of Warlock Flake. He was personally convinced that he had a case to investigate, but there seemed to be a missing link. Means? Opportunity? Motive? The three fundamentals of murder. What means had been employed to bring about the deaths? He didn't know. What opportunity had anybody to help the three men off their respective cliffs. There had been nobody close at hand in any of the three cases. There were guesses he could make, of course. The murderer could have hidden above each climb and dropped something—not a stone, that would have been noticed by watchers below. But what about sand or dust or a spray to blind the climber? The dead men were reported as having shaken their heads as if to rid themselves of dust . . . he decided this was not really a practicable idea either. To drop dust or direct a spray so accurately, just at the moment a climber had his eyes lifted would need a precision of aim unlikely of achievement. Poison? There had been post-mortems on the first two victims. No hint of toxic substances had been found. Besides, what toxic substance was there that could be guaranteed not to attack a man before he started a climb, but to strike him once he got on to the face after . . . how long? The man Bullock had mentioned half an hour, while Hawker had estimated thirty-seven minutes. Perhaps if he were to compare timings . . .

As to motive, he was even more in the dark. What constituted a motive in a place like this, full of highly intelligent people? Outside it would be sex, greed, jealousy, envy, hate . . . the usual run of human subculture that grows on the surface of the soup of society, turning it sour and mouldy. But here . . .

The pipe had burned itself out. The dottle gave a little warning sizzle that the end had come. He tapped it out carefully on the heel of one shoe and replaced it, bowl uppermost, alongside the white silk handkerchief in his breast pocket.

He was half way back to the main house when he heard his name called. A car had stopped on the drive opposite the end of the narrow paved path he was taking. Partington.

"Hello, doc! Just finished your morning rounds?"

"A couple of patients in the village. Neurotic wives of nuclear physicists. Trying to wean them off barbiturate sleeping pills."

"Succeeding?"

"To some degree. Hypnotics and tranquillisers are the bane of my life and the ruination of most others . . . why? What's up? Have I said something interesting?"

"Only if you can tell me my three dead climbers were on sleeping pills or any other form of medication."

"That horse won't start for you. I'll be breaking no ethical silence by telling you that none of them had ever had medicines of any sort while at the Centre and, furthermore, as it is my duty to give everybody here an annual check-up, I can tell you all three were pretty healthy specimens." He opened the nearside door of the car. "Here, get in. I can't sit blocking the drive. Come up to my office for a coffee."

"You're thrashing about," accused Partington when they were sitting in his consulting room drinking the coffee his nurse had brought in. "That's not like you."

Masters laughed. "It is, you know. In fact, I've just told the Director so. I always cast about. But I don't always do it in public when I want to make great threshing sweeps."

"Usually in the silence of your lonely room, eh? Why the performance this time?"

"I want to surprise somebody into doing something."

"Like jumping over your rope as you circle it?"

"I'm a little uneasy. There are coincidences, but no particular pattern that we have yet discovered. I'm here because of a series of coincidences. Three scientists die. All in the same way. All from the same Centre. All from the same Group within the Centre. I could go on wringing similar examples of a concurrence of events and circumstances without apparent causal connection out of these incidents. Every nerve in my body is screaming blue murder. But I haven't even established beyond doubt that there has been murder done, let alone the blue variety; and I have no idea as to who committed it. So I'm a bit off balance. Mostly I'm presented with a corpse and asked to discover who encompassed the death and how. If possible, why, too."

Partington grinned.

"You're a humbug. I can recall your sergeants telling me that you always go broody when you first start to fathom a case. You were broody when I saw you outside. You're broody now. Talking for the sake of it."

Masters waved a disclaiming hand. "Honestly, I'm still in the dark. What can possibly make three experienced climbers who are neither pushed nor poisoned, fall from three easy pitches? Answer me that one and I'll be a long way nearer solving the puzzle."

"I'd suggest drink," said Partington, "but I know these three weren't topers, and certainly no alcohol was found in the bodies of the first two. We'll know about Mailer when the reports come through."

"Did you speak to the doctor who was first on the scene?"

"I rang his surgery this morning. He was out delivering an infant. His receptionist said she would ask him to call me back."

"So I'm still marking time," said Masters.

"And you don't like it one little bit, do you?"

They congregated in the bar at lunchtime.

"The DI told us last night," said Masters, "that Hawker was very specific about the length of time which elapsed between Redruth starting his climb and his fall. He stated that the period was thirty-seven minutes, and Bullock said his attack of giddiness started after half an hour."

"Is it significant, Chief?" asked Hill.

"I don't know. But those are solid facts—two of the few that we have. We've been wondering what would cause these men to fall from cliffs. Men who were apparently one hundred per cent fit at the bottom, and yet feeble enough to fall off half way up."

"I get it," said Green. "If they all took about forty minutes to fall it would begin to look as though they had been poisoned at the bottom with something that takes that long to work."

"Right."

"Come on, Chief!" said Brant. "You're not asking us to start believing in unidentifiable South American arrow poisons are you? Those bodies had no toxic substance detectable at post-mortem."

"I'm only too well aware of that. I'm also aware that we're having to cast about for leads. This could be one. I want you to ask all the eye-witnesses for estimates of time between the victims leaving the ground and falling."

"You lads can do that," said Green.

Hill and Brant nodded. Masters went on: "I have discounted

hypnosis on the grounds that not only would it be difficult to find the opportunities necessary for putting men like that under unbeknown to them, but also because I understand that even under hypnosis it is virtually impossible to make a subject act in a way that he would not normally choose when not under the influence. But we do know that Silk took a swig at his water-bottle before setting out. We've seen a film of him doing it. And the DI was told last night that Redruth also drank from a bottle before starting his climb."

"Bullock, too," said Hill. "I can remember his exact words to me. 'I promise you I'd had nothing to drink except water from my bottle half an hour before.' "

"It's that half an hour which intrigues me," said Masters.

"Call it about half an hour, Chief. He was just chatting, not being specific."

"Near enough forty minutes," growled Green, "for somebody not watching a clock."

"So what have we got?" asked Masters. "Four men. Let us call them One, Two, Three and Four."

"Four?"

"Include Bullock who, according to his story, nearly bought it eight months ago. So, One is Silk, Two is Bullock, Three is Redruth and Four is Mailer."

"Paper," grunted Green to Brant. "Shove this down."

"Dizziness.

	One—as seen in the film and testified by Roslin.
	Two—self testimony
	Three—as testified by Hawker
"Timing—forty minutes.	Two—self testimony
	Three—testified by Hawker
"Drink from bottle.	One—as seen in the film
	Two—self testimony
	Three—testified by Hawker
"Same gear.	One—as seen in the film
	Four—as witnessed by Masters."

"Everything duplicated," announced Brant, and all men appear at least twice on the list except Four."

"To be absolutely complete," announced Brant, "there should be sixteen entries on the list. We've got nine."

"That's our job then," said Masters with some inward relief. "To fill the gaps. Not quite as big a job as it sounds, because if you leave out Mailer, number Four, we've got eight out of twelve. So, gentlemen, you have at least four spaces to fill."

"What about you?" asked Green.

"I'll deal with Mailer and a few other odds and ends."

"I want to have a look at Widow Twankey, don't forget."

"Right. Let the sergeants fill the gaps. They've got the list of eye-witnesses."

"We've already seen most of them," said Hill.

"See 'em again," grated Green. "This time you'll have the specific question of how long these chaps were on their cliffs before they fell."

"And dizziness?"

"Try to winkle it out of them."

"Wait a moment!" said Masters suddenly.

"Now what's up?" asked Green.

"Didn't Hawker say that Redruth was leaning over to his right when he fell?"

"I said he did last night," said Green belligerently. His memory was good enough to give almost verbatim reports of lengthy conversations, and even this small fact had not been missed.

"What about the film of Silk? He was outstretched to the right, too."

"Could be reasonable coincidence," said Brant. "I mean they've got to be either upright or leaning one way or t'other."

"That's right enough," said Hill, "but Bullock did say he was on a traverse, flat against the rock, leaning over sideways to the *left*."

"But he was *leaning over*," insisted Masters. "Find out from one of yesterday's witnesses exactly how Mailer was placed immediately before he fell."

"Right, Chief."

"I'd like some more beer," said Green. "Who's in the chair?"

He burped audibly and held out his tankard. "We're wasting good drinking time."

As Brant got the refills, Hill said: "I followed Bullock to Mrs Mailer's house this morning, so it looks as though his story about him being in cahoots with her is right enough. The trouble is, we've not seen him since. We've not been able to ask him any questions so far."

"I'd like his answers. He's our living witness."

"I told him he could meet you. Will you be about if he asks to see you?"

"I expect so. Somewhere inside the wire."

"You know what," said Green. "If that woman, Clay, keeps all that kit laid out like an army Q store, she probably gets people to sign for it when they draw it. If so, she should have a book of signatures."

"Which would tell us who had set number six on the relevant dates?"

"Why not?"

"Thanks for the tip. I'll tackle her about it."

His opportunity came very soon. Dorothy Clay came into the bar with Winter and two other men, both unknown to Masters. From where they were standing, they could hear her say: "My turn, I think. The usual for everybody?"

"At least she stands her corner," said Green. "If you've got to have women around it's as well to make sure they know the form."

"And what form!" said Hill. "She's got a pint of wallop for herself. The others are getting by on sherry and tomato juice."

"Cheers, chaps!" Dorothy Clay obviously knew the cries of yesteryear. And she knew how to drink deep. The level of the beer in her tankard fell by more than an inch at the first swallow.

"Excuse me," said Brant. "See you later."

Masters glanced at the door. Cynthia Dexter and Gerald Newsom—or so he supposed them to be—were coming in.

"Is that the sarn't's bit of capurtle?" asked Green. "She's not bad. Not bad at all."

"She'd suit you," agreed Hill. "She's not the skinny type."

"Get him away from her," said Green. "He can't compete with the matinee idol she's got in tow."

"Tell him yourself," replied Hill. "He's bringing them over."

"Sin?" asked Green after the introductions had been made. "That's not a bad name to have. It makes no demands. Nobody expects anything startling from a lass called Sin, an' then when they see somebody as luscious as you, the effect's devastating."

His three colleagues stared in surprise. Green being gallant was something new and totally unexpected. Cynthia seemed to sense she had called forth an unusual and infrequent compliment.

"How very nice of you! My ideas concerning policemen are changing rapidly."

"It's in her stars," explained Newsom. "Appreciative of authority. That's what they say about her."

"I'd like to be able to read the stars," said Green. "It'd be a great help in our job."

Newsom shook his head. "I'm not sure it would," he said seriously. "In fact, I'm thinking of chucking it in."

"Why?" asked Cynthia. "You only started your study about a month ago."

Newsom accepted his drink from Brant. Masters asked quietly: "Has something frightened you, Doctor Newsom?"

Newsom nodded. "It was a joke. I thought it would be amusing to do a serious study of a fatuous subject. . . ."

"As a form of rebellion against what goes on in the Centre?"

"You're a perceptive sort of character, aren't you?"

"I'm paid to be."

"Yes, well, I ran a cast on our three departed colleagues this morning."

"And?"

"They overlapped. It was rubbish. Absolute rubbish, but so near the truth. What I mean is, anybody could have written it all at any time, but there was something nasty about the sixth and eighth houses of all three."

"That's the second time I've heard houses mentioned in this context," said Green. "What's it mean?"

"Those parts of the charts dealing with specific aspects of life. In this case, health and death. The planets influencing these houses were pretty inauspicious. Saturn is death, you know, and Mars the sign of the knife. One or other figured in all three—not in exact opposition transit to their ascendants, but close enough to be uncomfortable in view of their deaths. Never a Venus or a Jupiter in sight, as it were. Nothing but what the guff calls unbenign influences. Now that's too near the mark for the likes o' me, rubbish or not."

"Don't meddle, son," counselled Green. "A palmist once refused to read my hand because I'd got a short life-line. I was in uniform at the time and there was a war on. A pal who was with me had a life-line that said he would live long enough to get a telegram from the monarch. She told him all about it. Three weeks later he was dead. There was an OHMS telegram all right —to his parents from the War House."

Cynthia Dexter turned to Brant. "You've never been to an astrologer, have you?"

"No."

"Thank heaven for that."

Green and Masters exchanged glances and moved away. "She's hooked him," growled Green. "She's beginning to take over his welfare."

"I came to the same conclusion."

"It won't work. Somebody's going to get hurt."

"Nothing to do with us. Let it run its course. Now, if you don't mind coming into the dining room, let's move. Doctor Clay has left her party and has gone in alone."

"You mean we could share her table?"

"As to that, I think we should have to wait for an invitation. But if she is eating alone, I could use the occasion as an excuse for introducing you to her."

Dorothy Clay made no move to invite them to join her table. She stood with a plate of food in her hand beside the seat she had chosen at an empty table and acknowledged Green mono-syllabically. It was Green himself who forced the point.

"Mind if we sit with you for a minute or two, Doc? While you have your grub? A bit of different conversation's a joy in a copper's life. An' a lady doctor of physics's somebody I've never met before."

"Oh! Yes . . . yes . . ."

"Fine." Green pulled her chair out. "Sit you down." He then took a seat himself. "You live in these barracks, yourself, do you?"

Dorothy Clay was evidently not prepared to start her meal in their presence, nor was she going to make the conversation easy. In fact it was hard work to keep the verbal ball rolling. At last Masters said: "Aren't you going to eat, Doctor?"

"I'll wait. A salad won't get cold."

Despite the chill reply, Masters went on: "In that case I'd like your opinion, Doctor."

"What about?"

"Your three dead colleagues."

"I know nothing about their falls. I was on all three expeditions, but I was miles away each time when they slipped."

"Quite. I wasn't going to ask you about their falls."

"No? I thought you were investigating murder."

"If murder has been done."

"I don't understand."

"There is nothing to say the three men were murdered. We have to establish that there was foul play before we can regard these incidents as crimes."

"What do you want my opinion on?"

"Just that. Were the three men killed by another's hand?"

"How can I say?"

"You knew their characters; their strengths and weaknesses; their climbing abilities; their worries and successes at work. As a trained scientist, an expert at summing up evidence, would you say they slipped by accident? Did they commit suicide? Were they over-confident in their ability? Were they drunk? Did they lose concentration? Were the pitches unsafe—slippery after rain?"

"I would have said that probably all those things contributed in differing degrees. One may have been suicide . . ."

"Which one?"

"I was speaking generally."

"I see. So you don't think they were murdered?"

"No. The idea is preposterous."

Green offered cigarettes across the table. "If you're not going to eat, have a fag." She accepted his offer. "One thing we can be sure of," Green continued as he lit the Kensitas she had taken, "and that is that their equipment didn't let them down."

"I think I can assure you on that score."

"That's right. The Superintendent here told me that Doctor Winter let him glance into your store room. Full of praise, he was, for the lay-out and neatness and so on. He said it showed you took pretty good care of things."

She blushed at the praise. "It is a simple system. The only practical one if you don't want all the gear just slung in a heap. It also ensures that by handing out complete sets nobody arrives at a camp or climb without some vital piece of equipment."

"Just like a well-run army Q store," agreed Green. "Everything in its place. Issued against signatures and chitties. Pretty fool-proof and it means you don't lose valuable stuff without knowing who's responsible for losing it."

Dorothy Clay blew out smoke and nodded agreement. She picked a speck of tobacco off her tongue with two fingers of the hand that held the cigarette.

"Don't tell me you make your colleagues sign for what they draw up," said Masters with a smile. "Issue ledgers and so forth."

"I make them sign. Yes. It's the only way. But I don't use a ledger."

"Oh?" Green sounded faintly disappointed.

"No. I had our printing department run me off five hundred little lists of what each set contains. Climbers sign one of these lists when they take gear. I hold the list until the gear is returned. Then they get their receipt back to destroy. That way I have no bookwork."

"A very efficient system," said Masters. "Can I get you some coffee, Doctor Clay?"

"No thank you." It was apparent the interview was at an end.

They rose to their feet as she drew her plate towards her. "I must hurry as I have to get back to the lab. I had only intended to be here for a few minutes."

"She's cagey," said Green, as they joined the queue at the serving counter. "Another who's hiding something."

"Frightened we suspect her beloved Doctor Winter, perhaps."

"That's what I thought. Trouble is, does she actually know something about him that she wants to keep from us, or is she just scared there might be something she doesn't really know, but suspects?"

"Not very helpful either way, is it?"

"It could be a pointer. Her attitude, springing from whichever source, strengthens our belief that Winter is involved, and that's damned helpful."

"Maybe. But I'd like a few solid facts."

"Hark who's talking! As often as not on a case like this when I ask for facts, you turn your nose up."

"True," admitted Masters, holding out a plate for a serving of vegetables. "But once the thing starts to point in a definite direction—a direction we've inferred from deduction rather than from material fact—then we need to confirm our beliefs by tangible evidence. Here we are, fairly sure of our ground, but with nothing to back us up. Say we do look hard at Winter. What are the means, opportunity and motive?"

Green scratched one ear and followed Masters along the serving counter. "There aren't any of 'em," he muttered.

"Quite. Can you even suggest how they were coerced into falling off mountains?"

"Short of poison or booze, no."

"Winter's opportunity?"

"Seeing he was miles away at each critical time, no."

"And his motive?"

"Well, now, that could be anything."

"Exactly. What are we to do? Take our pick?"

Green grunted unhelpfully. As they reached their table they saw that Hill and Brant were eating at the same table as Cynthia

Dexter and Gerald Newsom. Hill looked up and caught Green's eye, acknowledging that the time had come to get back to work.

"That youngster and his stars!" said Green. "You'd think he had something better to do with his time with all this female talent about."

"You pulled his leg about that palmist."

"No more than you pulled Clay's about us not knowing whether there is murder to investigate or not."

Masters grinned. "I didn't want to alarm her too much."

"Rubbish. You wanted to catch her off guard, to see if she would drop Winter in the fertiliser."

"Of course I did. Nor was I the only one. It was you who suggested she was Winter's mistress—not to her face, but to Toinquet."

"Do you deny it was a fair enough assumption?"

"No. But there is little point in making such an assumption—or rather, you wouldn't have made it unless you thought we could make some use of it. Otherwise, it is only of such academic interest as not to be worthwhile commenting on these days."

"This beef's tough. Came off a Patagonian ox, I reckon. Bet it chased many a groucho round a tree before it got clobbered for human consumption."

"You're evading my point."

"Of course I am. If I'd seen an opportunity to bring it up, I'd have been in there, punching. But she was like a clam. Sitting there not eating, with us questioning her! It just shouted police interrogation, and at police interrogations awkward questions are asked, so some people decide not to talk. The trouble was, it was not an interrogation—we couldn't put the forcers on her."

"What sort of an opening did you want?"

"What for? To ask a mature woman if she's a boffin's mistress? Or to get her to discuss Winter voluntarily?"

"The latter would be of more use to us."

"Maybe," admitted Green. "But if she's besotted with the bloke, we'd have got a pretty biased view."

"Would that have mattered?"

Green pushed his plate away. "Perhaps not—if we follow what

you're always spouting on about—turning even negative information into plus points. We've got it on good authority that he's good but not startling in his work. If she'd told us he was outstanding . . ."

"Go on."

"We'd have known she was laying it on."

"And her feeling for him would have been clarified."

"Up to a point. If we could have got a bit of pillow talk out of her—his aims and ambitions and how they've been thwarted, for instance—we might have learned he was jealous of these brighter, younger chaps who've died."

Masters nodded. "That was my point in trying to find out how successful the Group Six project is likely to be, and who is working on which theory. If those three men were all following one line of research which looks like turning up trumps . . ."

"You're right there. Bump 'em off an' claim the credit for yourself. The bloke who does learn how to shield those reactors is going to make a name for himself. If the boss thinks he's been passed over and it rankles, he could reckon this was his chance to put the record at what he thinks it ought to be."

"It's a thought. A word or two from Clay might have sufficed to turn idle speculation into something a little more concrete. Next time, perhaps."

Green grunted and got to his feet, but he stayed by his chair.

"She must know something. Else why was she so cagey about Winter and his bets?"

"The thought had occurred to me that Winter really did stop betting because he felt guilty about Silk."

"Meaning he has nothing to feel guilty about over the other two?"

"It could be."

Green sucked his teeth.

"I always knew this case was going to be a bastard."

Chapter 6

"SUPERINTENDENT MASTERS?"

The nurse who had brought the coffee into the consulting room in the middle of the morning was waiting as Masters reached the hall of the old house after lunch.

"Yes?"

"Dr Partington asked me to find you and I really didn't know where you were. I was asking John . . ." She nodded towards the custodian on duty.

"If ever you have to find me in future, always try Mr Toinquet. He usually knows where we are."

She smiled. "I'll bet he does." The tone gave Masters an inkling of how Toinquet's activities were viewed by the staff. Even by a pleasant young woman like this. She had a mature face. The sort that inspires confidence and sells goods on TV commercials. The youngish mum type who you just know will have nice kids, a nice husband and a nice house. He noticed she had nice legs, too, as she went up the stairs ahead of him. He decided that her uniform suited her.

Partington was busy filling in a number of record cards when Masters was shown in. He put them aside immediately.

"Dr William Brecon," said Partington, "presumably referred to locally as Bill the Pill, was the gent who answered the call for medical help when Mailer fell. He's one of the regular rescue team boys. He called through in his lunch hour."

Masters sat down. "To say what?"

Partington referred to his desk pad. "Multiple fractures. Left arm and left leg broken. Back of rib-cage smashed in. Head injury with brain damage . . ."

"How would he know that on cursory examination?"

"He diagnosed it by the nystagmus."

"Oh, lord!"

"Eye-rolling, to you. Mailer was lying on his back, seriously injured, but—as sometimes happens—his eyes were still open. Had his eyes been closed, Brecon might have guessed at heavy concussion. But as there was skull damage and the eyes were open, it was reasonable to suspect brain damage, especially as there was nystagmus which, itself, is a fair indication that the brain has copped it."

"Nothing more?"

"That's the lot."

Masters stretched his long legs. "Now where do I go for honey?"

"Up against it, are you?"

"Unless there was some sign of toxic substance in the body—yes."

"The pathologist's report will tell you that, but I'm doubtful whether there will be."

"Me, too. The two previous post-mortems haven't mentioned any. And this is the sort of case where I'm convinced I shan't be third time lucky in that respect."

"When do you expect to hear from the pathologist?"

"Later today. I've asked for a report from the doctor who attended him in hospital, too."

"The one who received him was probably the Casualty Officer. A youngster doing the Sunday stint. They're usually fairly inexperienced and always too overworked to pick up details such as you would like to hear. So don't expect too much from that quarter."

"I won't." Masters got to his feet. "Thanks for the help."

"If it was any help, you're entirely welcome."

Green had decided it was time to ask some questions about Toinquet, and to this end he thought he would question the guards at the main gate. As he approached the lodge, one of the uniformed security men came out to intercept him.

"You going out on foot, Inspector? It's a long way to the village."

Green took an instant dislike to the man and his manner of speaking, but in the hope that he would get something useful from him, he replied urbanely enough.

"Not going out, son. I've come to speak to you."

The guard's eyes showed wariness. That alone caused Green's old heart to sing. "Sorry, Inspector. No conversations allowed while on duty."

"You've got a mate inside, haven't you?"

"You're not allowed in there, either. Not to gossip."

"Look, lad, your oppo is on the phone right now to Toinquet. . . ."

The surprise in the guard's eyes showed Green he had scored an easy bull.

"Tell your boss I want to speak to you two. In the line of duty. Special exception to the rules."

"Stay here." The guard went into the lodge. He was back again almost before Green had selected a bent Kensitas and lit it.

"Nothing doing. Mr Toinquet says no exceptions."

"Thanks," said Green. "You've told me what I wanted to know, mate."

"Oh, yeah?"

"Yes. People who don't want to talk to a policeman investigating a murder—particularly Security chaps like you, in uniform— have some little secret to hide. And that's nice to know. When I tell my boss that the Security Corps has some reason for not co-operating with us, he'll take you lot apart. He's that sort of bloke. Nasty, suspicious type. And, of course, you'll automatically go on our list of suspects. . . ."

The guard was growing angry—visibly. This didn't appear to worry Green. He blew smoke out of his nostrils, sucked a tooth and glared. "If I know anything about running a place like this, the least breath of suspicion about the guards is the signal for wholesale sackings. Got a nice little quarter here, have you? I'll tell you what, buster, you'll find it a hell of a job getting another free roof over your head as an out-of-work. Houses come expensive these days."

"I shan't get sacked for obeying orders," growled the guard.

"Want a bet? Laddo, the law of this land says it is the duty of every citizen to co-operate with the police. Now you tell me Widow Twankey's trying to overrule the law. Thanks for that bit of info. You've dropped him in it good an' proper. So long, chum. Enjoy your last tour on stag."

Green turned and started to walk away.

"Here, wait a minute, you. I don't let anybody threaten me."

"Then p'raps you'll tell me what you're gunna do about it? Apart from the fact, of course, that I haven't threatened you—merely let you know the score."

The second guard appeared at the door of the lodge. He called across. "What's on, Len?"

"This cocky copper's threatening me."

"Is he now? Well, we've got powers of arrest inside these gates. How about giving him a bit of his own medicine?"

Green said: "You two are a ripe pair. Every word that comes out of your ugly mugs gives me more reason to take you apart. And don't think I'll forget that joke about putting me in your nick." He turned and stumped away, back up the drive. He was nearing the house when Hill and Brant joined him from a side path.

"We've seen everybody except Bullock," said Hill. "He's not been back to the Centre since he left this morning."

"So he's stayed with Mrs Mailer. She'd need somebody by her."

"I suppose so. But we've got nothing out of the others. They can't remember what kit Redruth had or how long it was after he started off that he fell. The only thing one of them can remember about him was that his water-bottle was leaking. He took it off the body together with all the other gup and put it in the coach for Clay to collect. He says the water ran down his trousers as he was carrying it over, so he pulled the cork out and emptied it."

"And he can't remember the number?"

"No."

"In that case . . . hey! I wonder if that club keeps accounts?"

"It has to," said Brant. "All government jobs do. They'll be consolidated in the Centre's welfare accounts if they were given grants from public money."

"General Office," said Green. "See if they've replaced any gear. If they haven't, and we look for a leaky bottle, or a set without a bottle . . ."

"No good," said Hill. "It'll only help us if it was number six, and we know number six was sound because Mailer was using it this week-end. He wouldn't have set off up a mountain with a hole in his bucket."

"Aye, you're right. Still, it's worth a try. But before you go, have you met Widow Twankey's understrapper yet? He must have a second-in-command of some sort."

"That's a thought," said Hill. "I've not met him. Probably it's his rest day."

"Why not ask Toinquet?" said Brant.

"I'll ask that secretary of his," replied Green. "She'll have the situation buttoned up."

Green was being heavily gallant.

"Miss Alice . . . I'm sorry to be so familiar, but that's the only name I know you by."

She looked over her spectacles at him.

"Alice will do, Inspector. Or Miss Dinwiddie, if you must."

"I was wondering where I could find Mr Toinquet's assistant. I've not met him yet, and I'd like a word."

"You will find him, I expect, at his house in the village." She scribbled on a notepad. "Here's the address and phone number."

"Thanks. But I'll not disturb him on his day off. I'll wait until he comes on duty."

"Then you'll wait a long time, Inspector. He's on a fortnight's leave."

"Starting when?"

"About three o'clock yesterday afternoon, I understand."

Green looked down at her. Her gaze was direct. He tried to read it. Her air of efficiency shone through, but he couldn't get what she was trying to tell him. Too neat, he thought. Too neat to be toothsome. But at her age, neatness and efficiency, amounting virtually to primness, were only to be expected, he supposed. Particularly in a career spinster.

She must have guessed his thoughts.

"You're summing me up, Mr Green. Assessing the woman in me."

Such frankness was a jolt, but Green was equal to the occasion. "Nothing was further from my thoughts," he lied, casting around for a reason. "I was wondering why an efficient PA like you, knowing everything that goes on, should only 'understand' that the leave of a senior security officer should start at three o'clock yesterday. I'd have expected you to be sure."

Her eyes twinkled in a smile.

"Sit down, Inspector." She indicated the corner of her desk. "You are a suspicious man, so let me explain. As yesterday was Sunday, I was not in the office . . ."

"But a fortnight's leave isn't taken on the spur of the moment. Surely you'd have booked it in weeks ago?"

"Quite right. I did. And then I had to delete it."

"Oh, why?"

"Because Mr Toinquet said it would not be convenient for Mr Mercer to be on leave just now."

"Any reason?"

"I think Mr Toinquet wanted a few days off himself."

"So that's why Widow Twankey was all dressed up with no-where to go when we arrived. He was ready for leave with a flying start, was he?" He looked down at her. "But yesterday afternoon he changed his mind and told Mercer he could have the original dates?"

"I assume that Mr Toinquet thought that he himself should be on the premises while you and your colleagues are with us."

"So he should, Alice. And so should his deputy. So, like me, you're wondering why Mercer should be sent off at all, let alone at three in the afternoon. If he had to be away, why not after duty? That's the usual time for leave to start, isn't't?"

She nodded. "I scented a mystery myself. But I can tell you no more than you've already heard."

"Ta, love. You've been a great help."

Her eyes twinkled behind her spectacles.

After leaving Partington, Masters wanted to think. Nobody at the Centre had offered him an office as an HQ. Crome had probably thought Toinquet would have arranged this, but the security man had obviously not thought it necessary. So, as he was on the first floor, and the various library rooms were close by, he decided one of them would afford him the necessary peace and quiet. He walked slowly along the corridor and entered the technical section room.

"A book, sir?" The librarian, now she knew him, seemed prepared to be friendly and helpful, but obviously considered her domain a place for reading, not thinking.

"Er . . . yes, thank you."

"Subject?"

He was at a loss as to what to ask for, but he didn't want to hurt her feelings or to became engaged in explanations for his presence. Then his recent conversation with Partington threw up the word he hadn't understood. "Not a subject, exactly. I'd like to check up on nystagmus." He spelt it out for her.

"Is that a physical phenomenon, sir?"

"In the medical sense."

"In that case we want the section on the principles and practice of medicine. If you would like to sit down I'll bring you what I can find."

He chose a seat at a table in the window while she riffled through book indexes. She brought him first one open volume, then another, and a third. Then she left him to get on with it.

He wasn't really interested in the written word, but he made some attempt to read. 'Continuous rolling movement of eyeball . . . aural nystagmus, lateral, jerking, rotatory . . .' The types and their causes were explained. He turned to the second book. 'Brain damage . . . lesions of the cerebellum—the inferior part of the brain—produces disturbances of the eye movements. Jerking nystagmus is commonly seen . . .' He continued to read for no good reason. 'Jerking nystagmus in the vertical plane generally indicates that the lesion is in the brain stem rather than in the labyrinth. In cerebellar lesions the nystagmus is more marked on deviation of the eyes to the side of the lesion . . .'

It was rapidly driving him to sleep. He read bits twice and made no sense of them. The lines danced. He tried to think, but found his eyes heavy.

"The tea trolley's outside, sir. Would you like a cup?"

The librarian's voice brought him awake with a start. He had no liking for institutional tea, but he thought a cup might serve to bring him fully awake.

"Thank you." He put his hand in his pocket. "How much?"

"Guests free," she said cheerfully, and went out into the corridor.

As he knew it would be, the tea was ghastly. Stewed and far from hot, but it served its turn.

He stood up. "Where shall I leave the cup?"

"Oh! Are you leaving?"

"Yes. I've read what I wanted. Thank you for your help."

"It's just that I've got some more information on nystagmus for you. You see, you said it was medical physical, which it is, of course. But I have here a recent article which is physical physical, if you follow me."

"I take it that you file in the physics section any medical paper which has a bearing on physics, is that it?"

"Yes. I thought I remembered getting one a few weeks ago. . . ."

He held out his hand. In the face of her pleasant and helpful attitude he felt he couldn't be boorish and refuse to accept the paper. He noted with gratitude that it was a small article occupying only two or three magazine columns. He returned to his seat, packed his pipe and was about to light it when he recalled that smoking is usually forbidden in libraries. With a sigh he picked up the paper.

Short or not, the article riveted him. He read it once, avidly, then a second time more slowly. Now was the time to think. Brain alert. All systems go. He forgot the probability of a ban on smoking. He lit his pipe and concentrated. The bits and pieces began to come together. Those facts still to be checked began to marshal themselves in his mind. Out of confusion came a pattern—conclusions from hints, conclusions from known facts, conclusions from conclusions . . .

He was astounded when the librarian said: "It's half past five, sir. I lock up now unless there is something else you would like."

"Good heavens! So late?"

"Was the paper any help, sir?"

"So much so that I'd like to borrow it, if I may. Would that be possible if I signed for it?"

"You can have it, sir. It's only a photocopy. I've got the journal it came from. February's *Nature*, isn't it?"

"That's right. Volume two four seven, page four oh four."

She smiled at him as he left the library. She didn't know it, but Masters felt like kissing her.

Green left Alice Dinwiddie and crossed the hall to the general office of the Centre. Hill and Brant, he was informed, were in the Senior Administrator's office. He was at liberty to join them if he so wished. He did wish.

"I'm Thorne." The Senior Administrator was a big man of about forty. Hair standing up in tight curls and greying. "I'm a bit of a misfit here—an ordinary civil servant. So when some of the excitement comes my way I'm ready to make a meal of it. Makes a change from chair-polishing."

"Nice of you to be so co-operative," said Green.

"Co-operative, but unhelpful."

"You haven't got the accounts?"

"Oh, I've got them all right. But they don't show any new equipment purchases. Nothing since the original capital invest-ment. And even those items were written off immediately for accounting purposes. So there's nothing I can tell you".

"Mr Thorne," said Green cheerfully, "you've given us what facts there are. Whatever has happened is fact—positive or negative."

"Perhaps I'd have been able to appreciate that better if I'd known what you were after."

Green shook his head. "We weren't after anything except facts. We can't just go after anything we think we'd like to see. It'd be nice if we could. Like you looking for a bit of surplus money over at the end of the financial year."

"The fact is that such a thing never happens."

"There you are then. Same with us. So we have to accept what's there. Right, we'll leave you in peace, Mr Thorne, and get on with our nosing about."

As soon as they were clear of the house, Green said: "I want to go into the village, so whistle up the car and let's get weaving."

"Where's the Chief?" asked Hill when Brant had gone for the car.

"God knows, and I don't suppose he cares. He's had it on this case."

"Who, the Chief?"

"Doesn't know whether he's coming or going."

"Is that a fact or simply an assertion?"

"Both, laddie. That's why we're in a hurry."

"To beat him to it?"

"And why not?"

"That'll be the day! If the Chief's all at sea, I don't reckon much to our chances of cracking it."

"Come along and see what we get."

"It's nice to meet a crowd of decent coppers," said Mercer.

"You're an ex-yourself?" asked Green.

"Nothing ex about it. Seconded here. I'm still serving. Inspector Mercer at your service."

It was a neat little semi. It was easy to see that Mrs Mercer took a great pride in it. And that Inspector Mercer took a great pride in his wife. With every reason. She was what Green privately designated as 'a pretty little thing'. She looked no more than a girl-wife.

"You wondering why I allowed myself to be pushed into this job?" he asked. "Because of Sue, here." He put his arm round her as she dealt with the tea tray. "Regular hours. The irregular variety were playing hell with our marriage, weren't they, my pet? Here, I've got office hours, with the occasional visit to the Centre in the middle of the night in my duty weeks."

"And he's not out facing demos every Sunday," added Mrs Mercer. "At least when he goes off I know he'll be safe and he'll be back inside a couple of hours."

"Very nice," said Green. "But it's not all so reg'lar, is it? I mean, this leave you're on. First you put in for it, then it was refused, now you've got it. . . ."

"I don't know why men can't run their affairs better," said Mrs Mercer, pouting prettily.

"Why the sudden change?" asked Hill.

Mercer frowned. "I've been asking myself that. Toinquet sprung it on me yesterday afternoon. I took it before he could change his mind again."

"That Toinquet!" said Mrs Mercer, perching on the arm of her husband's chair. "He's ever so hateful."

"Steady, love," said Mercer.

"Well he is. Look how he . . ."

"I said steady, Sue. Mr Green and the sergeants are here on a murder enquiry, not a gossip trail."

"Well, that was nearly murder, wasn't it? If it hadn't been for you and Doctor Mailer it would have been."

Green was sitting up and taking notice of this exchange between husband and wife. He glanced across at Hill and winked knowingly. The mention of Mailer and murder all in the same breath seemed to portend something of interest.

"That's got nothing to do with . . ." begun Mercer.

"Oh, but it has," said Green urbanely. "It seems you and Widow Twankey don't get on, Mr Mercer. Was there bad blood between Twankey and Mailer, too?"

Mercer sighed in exasperation. "It was about six weeks ago. We'd had a student protest at the gate. You know the crap. Banners saying 'We want bactericides not bacteria' and that sort of thing. That was on the Saturday afternoon. By tea-time the crowd had been dispersed by the local police, but Toinquet, quite rightly, ordered an increased security alert. It was getting dark then by five o'clock, remember, so on the Sunday we stood to at dusk again, just in case of trouble.

"Toinquet and I were both in the lodge, and there were two dog-handlers out with their animals between the wall and the wire."

Green nodded to show he understood. "The perimeter must be a long one."

"About one point six miles," agreed Mercer. "Hell of a distance to keep secure. That's why we have the fence electrified."

"Oh, yes?"

"About ten past five—remember we were in the control room in the lodge—the bell went, showing that a trip wire had been triggered. That meant that somebody had managed to get across the wall, but to me it meant that whoever had done it was a pretty clumsy customer. No professional would fall into the trap of touching an obvious trip wire. So I was fairly sure there was some kid acting the fool and the dog-handlers would get him right enough. I mean, notices telling people to keep out are like magnets to kids these days. They'll have a go just for the hell of it—not to pinch secrets."

"What did you do?"

"Nothing just then. Toinquet used the personal radio to set on the handlers. He was a bit excited. The day before could have been ugly, and you'll know him. The heavy hand every time. Hit and hit hard before asking questions. Anyhow, we've got a screen there which tells us if the electrified wire has been touched. There's not much current goes through—fifteen volts or some such. Just enough to activate the alarm."

"Somebody had touched it?"

"Yes. It might even have been the handlers, but it was proof enough for me we weren't being invaded. A pro would have that wire sussed out and avoid it like the plague. In fact, it's only there to tell us if kids are fooling about. What I'm saying is that the real boyos would never try to get in that way. They arrange for secrets to be carried out of the Centre if they want them. It's easier than going in for them, if you get my meaning."

"Perfectly, What happened?"

"Toinquet ordered the wire to be electrified with full power. I told him not to; that he'd probably be killing some young fool. But he went ahead. He pushed the bloody buss bar over himself."

"Then what?"

"Mailer was just coming through the gate. He bursts in and says he's just heard some kids howling in pain and fear out there, not far from the gate."

"He actually said kids?"

"Yes. Children's voices."

"So what happened?"

"I switched off the current. Toinquet was as angry as hell. Then Mailer and I went through the gate that leads into the gap and ran to where he'd heard the crying come from.

"He didn't have to tell me where to go. Have you ever heard a couple of youngsters badly burned as well as frightened out of their wits by a couple of Alsatians?"

"Blood-curdling?"

"I've a lad of five myself. I tell you, Mr Green, that if anybody ever harms that child there'll be payment taken. These kids were ten or eleven. Two of them. They'd got the jolt from the electricity, they'd been torn by the barbed wire, and they were too frightened to keep still with those guard dogs around. Of course they moved. Who wouldn't? And those dogs are trained to take anybody who doesn't stand perfectly still."

Brant shuddered.

"Jim had to tackle those dogs," said Sue Mercer. "Jim and Doctor Mailer. Their handlers had unleashed them miles away, so they weren't anywhere near to control them. The dogs had rushed ahead, you see."

"What the hell did you do?" asked Green.

"Mailer had a stick, so I reckon he crowned his brute. You see, the dogs had hold of the lads and would have had to leave go of them to come for us. I only had one hope. I got hold of the tail of one of them and twisted it as hard as I could go."

"What happened?"

"It let go of the lad. I hung on for dear life trying to stop it turning on me while Doctor Mailer swiped at it. He knocked it out at last."

"So both dogs were senseless?"

"It hardly seems possible, but yes. The handlers weren't very pleased, I can tell you."

"And the lads?"

"Both hospital cases. Both in a serious condition. Mailer and I carried them in and got Dr Partington. But you should have heard Mailer lambast Toinquet. 'Course he couldn't do anything not officially, because the safeguards are there to be used if there's anybody trying to break in. But he didn't let that stop him telling Toinquet what he was fit for."

"Was that the end of it?"

"Not quite. Next day Toinquet said I couldn't have this leave, and about two nights later the father of one of the lads—a farm labourer—gave Toinquet a black eye in the village pub. He'd heard, you see, that Toinquet was responsible for setting the dogs on and shoving the current through the fence."

"News gets around."

"They were a couple of nippers on a prank. We should have got them, stubbed their backsides and sent them home."

"So all this is what Widow Twankey wanted to stop you telling us?"

"Was that why he let Jim have his leave after all?" asked Sue Mercer incredulously.

"I think so."

"But I don't think that Toinquet got at Mailer," said Mercer firmly.

Green looked suitably dismayed. Hill caught his eye and stared unwinkingly.

"But there *was* bad blood between them," insisted Green.

"Certainly. And I'm not sure *I'm* going to last that long."

Sue Mercer gave a little cry of dismay when she heard her husband say this. Green got to his feet and patted her shoulder. "Don't you worry, love. We'll see he's all right."

Masters was using one of the private phone booths outside the ante room when Green and the sergeants ran him to earth after returning from the village.

"Trouble?" asked Green. "Something you didn't want somebody to know about?"

"I rang the North Wales Division. I asked them to send a detailed statement from the hospital casualty officer and anybody else who attended him, as well as the equipment he was using. In addition to the post-mortem findings we were already expecting."

"To come direct to you here?"

Masters nodded. "They'll send them by car tonight."

"What time will that be? It's six now."

"More than two hundred miles," said Hill. "And they'll have to wait for those statements. Say midnight at the earliest."

"Fair enough. There are one or two things still to do."

"Such as?" asked Green.

"See Winter and the other boffins in Group Six."

Hill looked at Brant. Masters was broody. The sure sign he was on to something. Brant nodded imperceptibly and then coughed gently. "Chief . . ."

"Yes? What is it?"

"I'll cancel this dinner engagement if you like."

"Don't do that. But I'd be glad if you'd use Doctor Dexter's car as I think we may need ours."

"Right, Chief."

"And Brant . . ."

"Sir?"

"By and large I don't think it a good idea to mix business with pleasure. Doctor Dexter has helped us tremendously already. Leave it at that."

"That's right, lad," said Green. "And don't let her baffle you with science, either."

Winter said, "Yes, I used to gamble. Not heavily, but often. When several of you are cooped up together in a lab you form a society much the same as any other. Mild betting, horseplay . . ."

137

"Horseplay?" asked Green. "Among senior scientists with all that apparatus about?"

"I should have said verbal horseplay. Not everybody was old, you know, and there is some pretty wit even among dedicated scientists. Limericks, puns, double entendre . . . the lot."

"And the betting?" asked Masters.

"I placed a bet with poor Silk—as a result of a friendly argument—that I could walk round to the top by the path route before he could make it by climbing."

"And?"

"I have never placed a bet since that day."

"You consider yourself in some way responsible for his death?"

"Logically, no. But I was still troubled. If there had not been a bottle of whisky at stake, would he have climbed alone?"

"That accounts for Silk being alone, perhaps. But why did Mailer climb alone?"

"I wish I knew. Certainly not on account of any wager I made with him."

"The whole of your research team knew of your bet with Silk?"

"I imagine the whole Centre knew. It was no secret."

Dorothy Clay said: "What would you do if your mere presence affected your wife's mental state adversely?"

"And that's why Doctor Winter stays away from his home and lives here in the Centre?" asked Green.

"Mrs Winter is looked after by her sister. She is not physically incapacitated, but her mental health is such that the sight of her husband causes whatever neurosis she suffers from to be exacerbated to a stage where her actions are entirely unpredictable."

"Meaning she blames him for something he did in the past which sent her up the wall?"

She stared at Green with distaste. He, for his part, was deliberately playing it on the aggro level to anger and thus destroy the control of his witness.

"She mistakenly connects him with the discovery and use of the atomic bomb and all the horror that conjures up. But Doctor

Winter has never harmed his wife or anybody else. She is the victim of illness. Mental disease, if you like. No act of his caused it."

"Has he ever thought of divorcing her? To remarry? Somebody with his own interests? On his own mental plane?"

Dorothy Clay pursed her lips in anger. "Get out, you bastard. Leave this room."

"Why? What have I said?"

She was on her feet, thrusting her face forward. "You have insinuated that he should leave her for me."

"Not at all. There are lots of lady scientists he might like to . . ."

"There aren't!" It was a hiss. "There aren't. Get out. You're hounding me . . ." The blow she aimed took him by surprise. He retreated through the door as she broke into tears.

Crome said: "I told you when you first came, Superintendent, that they are a *corps d'élite*, with all the drawbacks that can imply. An inbred society. I thought you recognised that fully when you told me this morning that nobody could cater for finely balanced minds."

'I did recognise it, Director. But to recognise that comparatively little may unbalance something teetering on a knife edge is not to know what that little cause may be. For instance, what may well be a tragedy to the ordinary man—say the loss of a hundred pounds—could well, I imagine, have no effect whatsoever on a high-grade physicist, no matter how poorly paid. He could well brush it aside as of no consequence."

"Oh, quite. There are some like that."

"So what would push them over the edge?"

Crome paused a moment before replying. "Without a doubt—and what I have to say can be proved by known instances—the most likely event to cause mental distress in my sort of people is professional mistrust or disdain."

"By other scientists?"

"Naturally. Lay opinion would count for nothing. But for his peers to pour scorn on his results or ideas is—to use an over-worked word—traumatic to a scientist. Mental trauma ... even psychic trauma, has been caused in this way."

"Do I take that to mean that the shock causes injury to the subconscious mind and produces a lasting emotional effect?"

"I don't think I can put it better than that. But may I ask if a case of psychic trauma is what you are considering as a possible motive for murder?"

"I think that is what I must do. The alternative would be malicious."

"Thank you for that, at least."

Mayes, the chief lab technician of Group Six, said: "Of course they laughed. They all did. But some were kinder than others. Silk proved it wrong mathematically. Redruth and Bullock knocked their heads together over it and decided that it was hampering their work. They were, in fact, prepared to go above Winter's head and claim that time, money and equipment were being wasted. But Redruth died before they could get their case in a presentable form. After that, Bullock didn't seem to care so much."

"And Mailer?" asked Masters.

"I don't know about him. He was a pretty quiet sort of chap just so long as things were as he thought they should be. But when he got his dander up, he could be the very devil. I know. He's blasted me before now when things haven't been ready for him and it's been important that they should be."

"Could he have got cross with Doctor Winter at any time?"

"Most likely. But he'd do it in the Doctor's office, not in public. He always came into my cubby hole if he wanted to complain to me about anything my crowd had done wrong."

"Your crowd?"

"Technicians and lab assistants. My responsibility."

Hill and Green ran Drew to earth at his home in the village.

"Of course I didn't complain. What was the use? I'm getting out."

"But the situation was pretty bad from your point of view?"

"Incredibly bad. You know we have a number of scientific assistants—not lab assistants—but qualified junior people? They're there to do some of the routine, to leave us free to get on. It is hell's own delight trying to get an hour of their time. The consequence is that our projects are held up—months behind schedule. Silk raved about it openly. Rutherford was for getting us all to sign a protest."

"But you did nothing?"

"I steered clear. I take the point of view that nobody can tell what may eventually spring from apparently wild ideas. So I'll play no part in suppressing them."

"Yet you're getting out."

"Not because of lack of freedom. Lack of facilities and assistance caused by too much freedom."

"You mean there should be more money allocated for the activities of Group Six?"

"There's a hell of a lack of direction. There needs to be a firm hand on the tiller."

"Look, Superintendent," said Saunders, "the chap who first put tags on bootlaces made a fortune. Good luck to him. Simple ideas are the best. But everything is comparative. The world today is complex. Simplicity is a matter of degree. But it's still there to strive for. I can feel it in my bones when we start stepping outside the bounds of simplicity. And under Winter this is what has happened. It explains why he, as an able scientist, never quite made the top. He has no sixth sense which says thus far and no farther. He cloaks this attitude under the guise of diplomacy or as support for freedom of thought—which no scientist would disagree with as long as there were legitimate aims in mind. But science is a discipline—in every sense of the word. Winter's team is in disarray, and those who have dared to say so are gone. Dead. And now you're here. My hope is you'll salvage something for us from the wreck."

At nine o'clock Masters was called to the phone outside the ante room where he, Green and Hill had been sitting after a hurried supper.

"Chief," said Brant's voice, "Bullock's here, drinking himself stupid. If you want to get any sense out of him tonight, it's got to be now. Do you want me to bring him in?"

"No. So long as he's turned up, that's fine. You return to your date. We'll be there ourselves, shortly. Leave it to us."

As Hill drove them to Pottersby village, Green said, "I can't see what the rush is. I was just going to have a drink."

"We're going to a pub."

"Oh, aye! So we are. But it's cheaper in the Centre."

"I'll buy you one. They don't come cheaper than that."

"OK. But what's your hurry? We're no nearer to pinning the job on Winter than we were yesterday at this time."

Masters didn't reply. Inside The Bull he saw Brant, who was taking coffee in the lounge.

"He's in the small bar to the right, Chief."

"Thank you. Good evening, Doctor Dexter. Have you had a successful evening.

"Not very, Superintendent."

"I'm sorry to hear that. What's gone wrong? Food no good? Sergeant Brant's company dull?"

"Far from it. It has all been very nice. But you asked me if it had been successful."

"And?"

"I haven't been able to persuade Sergeant Brant to become just plain Mister Brant."

"I see. And I told him not to mix business with pleasure."

She stood up. "Don't worry. I admire him for it."

"And that's as far as it's gone?"

"Unless you count the fact that my parents live only a few hundred yards from his, and when I visit my home next week I shall call on his mother."

"I'll make sure he has the day off."

"Why not the week?"

"Suffering cats," said Green as they left her. "She knows what she wants, that one. And gets it. And what do we get?

Flapper sergeants getting hitched to top-grade doctors of science! Wouldn't it root you?"

"Doctor Bullock?" asked Masters of the lonely, morose figure sitting in a corner of the bar.

Bullock looked up wearily.

"My name is Masters."

"The boss copper?"

"That's right. I have Sergeant Hill here with me. You remember him? And Detective Inspector Green. Can we give you a lift to the Centre?"

"Not yet. I'm still just sober enough to see three of each of you."

"Another drink?"

" 'sgenerous of you. Whisky."

Masters brought the glasses over.

"Here's tears, doc," said Green. "First tonight."

"I'm pleased to say it's far from being my first."

"Doctor," said Masters, sitting beside him. "You're blaming yourself, aren't you?"

" 'Course I bloody well am. How do I know Clive Mailer didn't find out about Marian and me and chuck himself off that face because of it?"

"Mailer would never have reacted like that. He'd have created hell. I've good evidence to prove that. He had his say with Toinquet, Mayes, Winter and various others at different times. And he always went straight to the fountain head. If he'd known you and his wife were spending week-ends together in his absence, he'd have told you in no uncertain manner. Rest assured of that."

"You're certain?"

"You know I am. You're feeling pretty disgusted with yourself. Well, that's natural. Just don't let your disgust include Mrs Mailer. The best recompense you can make to your friend is to see that his wife is looked after."

Bullock nodded. Masters seemed to have cheered him up slightly. "Don't worry on that score. If she'll have me permanently after a suitable interval . . ."

"Splendid. Now just one point you can help us on, Doctor. On the day you yourself nearly fell from a mountainside, what was the number of the set of gear you borrowed?"

"Number? How the hell should I know? After all this time? One set's just like . . . no, wait a minute. I always used to have five. That's right. The regular climbers staked a sort of claim on a set each and left it adjusted from week to week. An' then that last time Dottie said I had to have some other set because something had happened to number five. Rucksack torn or something."

"But you don't remember the number of the replacement set?"

"Haven't a clue. But I remember the bloody water-bottle sprang a leak. By the time I got to the bottom I looked as if I'd wet my pants."

"Thank you," said Masters. "I'm grateful for your help."

"Not much help if I couldn't remember the bloody number, was it?"

Masters smiled. "Shall we take you home? I'll send you out in my car in the morning to collect your own."

The police car from North Wales arrived at twenty past one in the morning. Masters, waiting up for it, spent less than half an hour reading the reports and inspecting the gear. Then he put in a call to the hospital in North Wales and held a few minutes' conversation with a very sleepy consultant surgeon.

After that, he went to bed.

Chapter 7

IT WAS HALF past nine on Tuesday morning. There were
seven of them sitting at the round table in Crome's office. Masters
had invited Toinquet and Partington to be present in addition
to the Director and his own three colleagues.

The sun had at last broken through the grey skies of the last
three days. There was an air of contentment about the meeting as
if everybody sensed that the tension was about to be relaxed.
As if to emphasise this, Green placed a new packet of Kensitas
on the table, while Crome rang for a coffee tray. The fire blazed
comfortingly and Masters, who was a devotee of Charles Lamb,
was reminded of the opening lines of the essay 'Mrs Battle's
Opinions on Whist': 'A clear fire, a clean hearth, and the rigour
of the game.' Only this time it wasn't a game, but a chase. A chase
he had successfully completed and about which he was now
prepared to report.

"I have to report," he began, "three successful murders and one
attempted but unsuccessful one."

"You've definitely established that they were murders?" asked
Crome, handing round coffee and asking the question much as a
committee chairwoman might enquire of her colleagues whether
there were enough tables for the tea-tent at the village fete.

Masters nodded. "Beyond doubt."

"Who was the subject of the attempted murder?" asked
Toinquet.

"Doctor Alec Bullock." Masters paused to allow the ripple of
comment that this announcement called forth to die down.
"Gentlemen, I am fully prepared to answer questions, and I would
like you to ask them, but I think many of the answers will become
clear as I go, so if I could ask you to hold back—except to

clarify points—you may find my report the more coherent for your abstinence. Bear with me, please, as I am trying to recount a complex narrative."

"Fair enough," said Crome.

"Thank you. Our first task, you will remember, was to establish that multiple murder had, in fact, been done. I have said categorically that we have established this. And so we have, to the tune of identifying the murderer and completing a case against that person. But our reasons for asserting murder are quite simple. In fact, in one word, similarities. Exact similarities in every case.

"I have here a film which shows Doctor Silk immediately before his fall. A moving film which shows him leaning sideways on the cliff face and shaking his head in some distress as if to clear his eyes of dust or grit. Our enquiries show that each of these men seemed to be moving their heads as if to clear their features or their senses—from dust or, as one witness put it, soap in the eyes. And at the time they were all seen to be doing this, they were moving or leaning sideways. Without exception.

"I see that this puzzles you, but you don't appear to find it significant. Perhaps one other fact will impress you. All the men who fell did so after being on their respective mountains for about thirty-five or forty minutes."

Masters paused. There was little reaction from his audience who sat there quietly staring at him. He felt slightly irritated by their apparent lack of interest. He hadn't got them with him—yet. Like most speakers in a similar position, he forged ahead.

"More materially, each of those men, with the possible exception of Bullock, was definitely using equipment set number six. All Bullock could tell us was that he was not using his usual gear—number five set. So there is the possibility that he, too, used number six; and I confidently believe he did, as I will try to show later."

The material fact hooked them. Climbing gear is tangible. Faulty gear? Was that the answer to the problem? Masters was pleased to get the reaction. Crome made as if to ask a question, but refrained. Toinquet nodded as if to show that he could appreciate that here was a point of importance. Partington actually muttered something about having wondered, earlier, whether their gear had failed the three dead men.

"The last similarity we have been able to prove conclusively is that each of the first three men took a pull at his water-bottle before starting the climb. I have no witness prepared to swear that Mailer did so, but it is, I believe, highly likely that he did take a drink at that time."

"Quite natural," said Partington, forgetting the promise of silence. "A drink and a nervous pee."

"That, too. At least in some instances. Those are the similarities I spoke of, gentlemen. I'll list them again. The same time spent on the rock-face; the same gear; the same canted-over position; the same drink; and the same signs of distress immediately prior to falling. Put them in any order you like, apportion them whatever significance you like, but the fact will still remain that there were five multiple coincidences which, added to the fact that all the men were senior scientists from the same group in the same Centre, make me certain that murder has been done."

"Astounding," said Crome. "So many indications must be conclusive—I regret to say. More coffee anybody? There's still some left, but we seem to be a bit short of milk."

"What about you, Widow?" asked Green. "Have you any objections?"

"What to?"

"The conclusion that there were three murders."

Toinquet shook his head. "Not if what the Super says is true. But don't forget most people were convinced it was murder before you people started to look around for the bits and pieces we've heard about so far."

Hill bristled. "What's that about if what the Chief says is true? Are you suggesting he's making it up?"

"No, no. Nothing like that. But it's very circumstantial."

"Not a bit of it," said Partington. "Any research scientist in this Centre, given a battery of facts like that, would consider he had proved a point. Is that not so, Director?"

"I would certainly postulate on such evidence and then seek to prove beyond doubt, which, I imagine, is exactly what Mr Masters has done and proposes to recount to us now."

"If you please," said Masters. He led off again. "In none of the bodies was there any toxic substance. Yet I could not disregard the fact that each man, about forty minutes after drinking from a water-bottle, and while carrying out a move that any mountaineer does quite frequently—that is, leaning to the right or to the left—showed signs of physical distress and then lost his grip and fell—all, that is, except Bullock whom we shall mention in more detail later.

"These facts convinced me that each of those men had ingested some noxious substance that took about forty minutes to work. But if so, whatever substance it was, immediately disappeared from the body. This seemed impossible outside the realms of the old undetectable poisons in which I am not a great believer.

"The poison—if such existed—could not have been excreted by normal bodily functions, because two of the men were dead before there was the possibility of this happening."

"You were up a gum tree there," said Partington.

"Until you helped me down," replied Masters.

"I did? How?"

"You asked—on my behalf—for a personal report from the doctor who was first called to Mailer—on the old-boy basis. Nothing in the report was unexpected by me, except the mention of nystagmus due—according to the doctor who made the report —to brain damage. Do you recall explaining it to me?"

"I remember."

"Nystagmus is an involuntary oscillating movement of the eyeballs in which they repeatedly turn slowly in one direction and fast in the reverse direction. The medical profession doesn't call it horizontal nystagmus, but I think we might do so to distinguish it from the other sort—jerking or vertical nystagmus. Is everybody clear on that?"

Nobody replied, so he assumed they understood him fully.

"The great thing about nystagmus is that it can be due to a variety of causes. For instance, with brain damage, the resulting nystagmus is of the jerking variety, whereas a person who has drunk too much alcohol—and is not used to doing so—will get a form of horizontal nystagmus, generally referred to in medical circles as PAN, I believe, Dr Partington?"

"That's right. Short for Positional Alcohol Nystagmus, because it only occurs when the head is held in certain positions when lying down."

"Is that absolutely right?"

"I believe so."

"Wouldn't it be more accurate to say when the head is held in certain positions relative to gravity?"

"Oh, yes, I suppose it would. But for all practical purposes when dealing with drunks, it happens when they are lying down with the head held right or left side down."

"Thank you. Gentleman, I am not suggesting that the three dead men were in a state of alcoholic intoxication when climbing. Far from it. It would have been better for them had they had a slug of brandy before setting out, for it was brandy that saved Alec Bullock. However, more of that later.

"To return to PAN. A drunk, with his head held right side down will evince nystagmus with his eyes turning fast to the right, slowly back to the left, fast to the right, and so on. This type is called 'to the right', named after the direction of the faster movement. When the drunk's head is to the left, the nystagmus is 'to the left'. In other words, nystagmus due to alcohol is fast in the direction of the cheek that is down or, more reasonably to laymen, fast downhill—as if pulled by gravity."

"You're labouring this point," said Toinquet.

"Because I want to be sure you understand what I have yet to say."

Partington looked across. "Yesterday you didn't know what nystagmus meant. Today you can give a lecture on it."

"All part of the service," said Green airily. He selected a Kensitas from the new packet without handing it round. "His mother was frightened by a rabbit, now he's for ever pulling them out of hats."

"Shall we push on? PAN is caused, after alcohol, by the action of gravity. That is why I was so particular to establish this point with Dr Partington, and because there is, in the ear, something called the vestibular apparatus which, as most people know vaguely, is the organ of balance for the whole body, and is not affected by gravity. This last point, too, is important.

"I'll try to explain this bit quite simply. In the vestibular apparatus there are sensory receptors and three semicircular canals. And it is these canals which cause nystagmus. Floating in each of these canals is a cupula—a sort of little ball which behaves like a buoy at sea. The liquid in the canals, in which the cupulas float, is called endolymph. The cupula is normally moved by movements of the endolymph, just as a buoy is moved by the sea. These movements of the endolymph result from angular accelerations—that is by movement of the head from side to side. But because the cupula has neutral buoyancy, it is not moved by linear accelerations—which are the movements you make when you look up or down— and so they are not affected by gravity."

"That's why, if you turn round and round rapidly, you lose your balance," said Partington. "But you can nod your head as much as you like and only get a crick in the neck without getting dizzy."

"Quite. But here's the important point. Because of their proximity to blood capillaries, after somebody has taken a lot of alcohol, the cupulas acquire alcohol more rapidly than their surrounding endolymph. In other words, the alcohol gets into the blood stream quicker than it gets into other body fluids. The cupulas thereby lose their neutral buoyancy, because alcohol is less dense than water. They therefore float high enough to be affected by gravity until the alcohol concentration in the endolymph in turn rises sufficiently to restore neutral buoyancy. Therefore, if you are very drunk and you get your head down and turned on one side, you can get strong sensations of bodily rotation, dizziness and nausea, together with motion sickness. I imagine most drunks, when put to bed, have experienced this."

"Good lord!" said Crome. "Imagine a drunk on a cliff face."

"But Masters said they weren't drunk," objected Toinquet, "and they wouldn't be lying down if they were on a cliff-face."

"If they were upright on a cliff-face they might be OK, admittedly. But the Superintendent has stressed that they were canted over."

"Right, Director. But he also stressed they weren't drunk. So what's he getting at?"

"Not drunk on alcohol, at any rate," said Masters.

"What else is there?" asked Partington. "Except possibly hallucinatory drugs or some such—and the post-mortems showed that this was not so."

"Heavy water," said Masters. "The stuff there's gallons of in Group Six."

"Drunk on heavy water?" asked Toinquet incredulously.

Masters nodded.

"I've never heard of this," said Partington.

"A very recent study," said Masters. "Your library, quite naturally, has a bias towards physics rather than towards medicine, so the paper was filed under heavy water and not under nystagmus. That's why you would miss it."

"How does it work?"

"It works in exactly the opposite way from alcohol, but the results are the same. Where alcohol is less dense than the endolymph, heavy water is much denser. After ingestion of heavy water, the cupula takes it up more quickly than the surrounding endolymph—just as with alcohol. But where alcohol causes the cupula to float higher, heavy water causes it to sink—with all the same results of losing neutral buoyancy. Whoever has drunk the heavy water eventually suffers from dizziness, sickness, etcetera, but particularly when keeling over into a lateral position—just as the drunk gets the same symptoms when lying down."

"Such as when leaning sideways on a cliff?" asked Crome unhappily.

"Exactly. But here is the point. Where PAN is, as I explained earlier, to the right if the right cheek is downwards and vice versa with the left cheek, heavy water nystagmus is in exactly the opposite direction. For obvious reasons. If positive buoyancy causes nystagmus to the right, even the layman can appreciate that negative buoyancy will cause it to be to the left."

"How does the direction affect these people on the mountain?" asked Crome.

"In itself, not at all. They suffered from dizziness, sickness, vertigo and nausea when they canted over, and they fell to their deaths. But where the direction of the nystagmus has helped us is in establishing that heavy water was, in fact, the culprit.

"Dr Partington had a call from his colleague in North Wales who had diagnosed brain damage because he saw nystagmus. Yet the post-mortem on Mailer did not confirm damage to the cerebellum—the lower part of the brain which, when damaged, causes nystagmus. So, what had caused the eye movement the doctor had observed? Alcohol? Or heavy water?

"I called the hospital and spoke to the surgeon. He had used electro-oculography to observe the movement, simply because Bill the Pill had suggested brain damage. Please understand that the surgeon was only interested in the nystagmus in so far as it was a symptom of brain damage. He was in a hurry to try and save a life, and he was not interested in causes other than those he could alleviate. So he ignored the nystagmus entirely once he'd established that the injury was elsewhere. However, when I telephoned him and asked for the direction of the nystagmus, he was able to recall—to his own great surprise—that the nystagmus was to the right when the head was left side down. I suspect that he had subconsciously noted this and the knowledge had been niggling away at his mind without his being able to identify it. The point is, gentlemen, that his information confirmed heavy water nystagmus of a particularly vigorous type."

"I take my hat off to you," said Partington. "Not one doctor in a thousand would know the effect of drinking D_2O."

"What about the similarities of timing of onset?" asked Crome. "You made great play of that earlier."

"Because they were so coincidental, Director. The paper I read describing the clinical trial stated that eye movements in all subjects had started within half an hour of drinking heavy water and the effects lasted until nearly eight hours later. But those subjects were lying down. So I had to assume that the first significant lateral position taken up by each man after being on the mountain-face for thirty minutes would cause the onset of dizziness."

"Which they tried to dispel by shaking their heads?"

"I think so. And in so doing, I assume, making their state even worse. All except Bullock, that is. He is a bit of a heavy drinker. He carries a flask of brandy on mountains. When he felt himself getting woozled, his natural recourse was to his flask."

"Got it!" said Partington. "The alcohol cancelled out the effects of the deuterium oxide on the cupulas."

"Quite right. The positive buoyancy induced by the alcohol neutralised the negative buoyancy induced by the heavy water. Restored almost neutral buoyancy, in fact, so that the dizziness was almost conquered and Bullock was able to make his way down in safety."

"Dear lord!" breathed Crome. "It's . . . it's almost beyond belief. And you say they all drank heavy water before they started to climb?"

"From the same water-bottle, Director. Number six."

"Which someone, presumably, had filled with heavy water in each case."

"Just so. My information is that a mere one hundred grams of heavy water will produce this intoxicating effect."

"A good mouthful, that's all," said Partington. "Bearing in mind how much denser than ordinary water the D_2O is."

"But," expostulated Toinquet, "why should they drink this heavy water? D_2O the doctor calls it. Even I know that ordinary water is H_2O. Wouldn't they know the difference?"

"The two are virtually identical in taste," said Crome. "And in looks. Possibly D_2O tastes a bit like distilled water—a bit lifeless—but nothing more. The only thing which might give the game away is the weight of the water-bottle, and that problem could easily be overcome by not filling it completely."

"Thank you," said Masters. "It all began with Doctor Silk.

He went up the mountain alone as the result of a wager with Doctor Winter."

"Don't tell me Winter . . ."

"Director, please! I think the bet was fairly common knowledge. Particularly in Group Six. Thus was the opportunity created. That bet probably sparked off the whole sequence. But it wasn't Winter's fault. It takes two to make a wager. But once the method used had worked so effectively in Silk's case, it was only a matter of time before it was used again and again. The perpetrators of such crimes have a habit of repeating themselves."

"But why? For what possible reason?"

"Doctor Winter himself gave us the clue, Director. In your presence he told me that in his small way he needed to be a diplomat in order to keep the peace between factions within his own group. He said categorically that he had to offer support, when needed, to alternative approaches which even he, himself, did not view with particular favour."

"I remember him saying that."

"Director, I must tell you that Doctor Winter's attitude, admirable as it may sound, has been the cause of great dissension in his Group. Where he was prepared to be diplomatic, other dedicated scientists were not. Many of them were, and are, openly critical of the lack of firm direction and the dissipation of the Group's energies in following so many lines of approach—particularly as some are so unpromising as to be clearly seen as dead ends before they were embarked on."

Crome grimaced as though sceptical of this. Masters carried on.

"I have a witness who states that Redruth and Bullock were preparing to approach you over the head of Doctor Winter to clarify the situation. Redruth died before they had their case for you fully prepared."

This time Crome looked dismayed.

"Other witnesses state that Silk was openly critical. Mailer is thought to have tackled Winter in private. Drew is resigning because of the difficulties he encounters. Rutherford is getting up a petition . . ."

"Please stop," said Crome. His face had a determined look. "You can leave this to me—now I know of it. But of what in particular do they complain?"

"What Doctor Winter described as the ultra-violet school."

"Doctor Clay's project?"

"Her colleagues are unanimously of the opinion that her theory is a non-starter. And have even proved it so. But as Doctor Clay works alone, she makes use, of necessity, of much more than her fair share of the juniors and technical assistants. She is Deputy Leader of the Group and such domestic arrangements are in her hands, so it is difficult for the others to alter things. This is apparently hampering unduly what is likely to be more fruitful work. Criticism has been rife and often outspoken. But, as Doctor Saunders put it, 'Winter's team is in disarray, and those who have dared to say so are gone. Dead.' And it is widely appreciated among those scientists that there is what we can only describe as a special relationship between Winter and Clay. . . ."

"Which you think accounts for his diplomatic support of projects he doesn't believe in?"

"Precisely. I repeat, criticism has been harsh and outspoken. You, yourself, spoke to me of psychic trauma where there is criticism of professional work. Think how great this trauma must be in a paranoic personality, and the length to which it will drive the unfortunate owner."

"To the mass murder of those who criticise?"

Masters nodded.

"Doctor Clay was the scientist who suffered. . . ."

"You mean Dorothy Clay killed those men?"

"I do."

"Unbelievable! Have you any proof to substantiate that she, and she alone, did it? I mean, you have shown the means employed to kill them, but . . ."

"We have the proof. Doctor Clay looked after the climbing gear. She very carefully obtained two water-bottles for set number six. We found one in her room immediately after she left it this morning. The other I received last night with Mailer's other belongings. I had wondered how she would get rid of the excess heavy water—that in the water-bottle which had not been drunk on each occasion. Bullock was very useful to me here. He remembered that by the time he had got to the bottom of the cliff his water-bottle had sprung a leak and he felt—as he put it—as if he had wet himself. The bottle had not sprung a leak. One of the number six bottles—the one we found in Clay's room—is sound. The one we got from Mailer's body has a small, neat hole drilled in the base. You will recall that army water-bottles are covered in felt. I imagine that Clay unstuck the felt on the bottom each time and plugged the hole with gelatine or some such substance which is slowly soluble in heavy water, and then replaced the felt. Bullock's story is confirmed by Doctor Roslin who was himself wetted by Silk's water-bottle after the first fall.

"To all intents and purposes, she would have issued a sound bottle to her intended victim. She would take along the heavy water in another container. She would transfer the heavy water just before the day's business started, and substitute the charged bottle for the one already filled with pure drinking water and strapped on to the gear."

"Wouldn't that be risky?"

"Would it? Two little buckles to undo and fasten again? If caught in the act she could say she saw one side was loose and was just tightening it up as she didn't want to lose any of her precious gear, etcetera, etcetera. And, of course, we don't know how many times she went out prepared to put her plan into action and came home foiled because the necessary opportunities did not arise. She was successful only four times in over a year!"

"Of course. I'm not thinking clearly at the moment."

"She needed to get rid of the residue of the heavy water—just in case somebody should suspect the water-bottle. After so long—say forty minutes—the gelatine plug would have dissolved, and the contents would then leak away. Could anything be more natural than a water-bottle which had been strapped to a fallen climber leaking after he hit the ground? Nobody would be surprised. In Bullock's case it leaked and wet his trousers. In Silk's case it wet Roslin. In the case of the others it would seep into the ground."

"She'd got it all thought out then," said Toinquet, "even though she was mad."

"Mad?" said Green in disgust. "She's as mad as a hatter. And not only over her science project. Over men, too. She's run poor old Winter something rotten. Mothered him, petted him . . . but she didn't pet me. She took a swing at me last night—and connected."

"She did what?" asked Crome incredulously.

"DI Green went along to question her. We had to be sure exactly what her relationship with Winter was, She objected so strongly that the DI was left in no doubt that she regarded Winter as her own. When he made his view clear to her, she assaulted him. He withdrew without retaliating."

"Poor old girl!" said Partington. "What now? Are you going to arrest her?"

"I have no choice." Masters turned to Toinquet. "I instructed your guards to stop her if she attempted to leave the Centre and to inform me direct. Similarly, the Custodian in the laboratory complex is to inform me if she attempts to leave the Group premises."

Toinquet started to protest at orders being given to his men without his knowledge, but he caught Green's belligerent eye and thought better of it.

"But you can't arrest me. I'm an important scientist. The government won't allow you. My research . . ."

"The government will give you all the time in the world for research, where you're going," said Green.

"Oh, will they? But I shall need assistants."

"There'll be assistants, too. Bags of 'em."

"That's good. So long as they're men. I find male assistants so much more pleasant to work with."

"I've noticed they all fall for you."

"Talking about falling," said Green an hour and a half later as they were on their way back to London, "what about Doctor Sin?"

"What about her?" asked Brant.

"Well . . . I mean, you can't be in one place while she's in another. Too much like old Winter and his missus to be comfortable."

"We don't intend to be," said Brant. "As there doesn't seem to be much likelihood of promotion in the force, I might as well get out."

"Don't do that," said Masters. He looked across at Green. "Don't you think that if Toinquet were to go, and Inspector Mercer were to take his place as Security Chief at the Centre, there'd be quite a nice opening for an intelligent young copper as his second-in-command?"

Green said: "I'm way ahead of you."

"Really?'

"Yeah! Last night, after I'd heard that story about Widow Twankey, I did a bit of phoning. It's remarkable how much harm one can do by asking just one simple question about somebody's suitability for the job he holds."

"Especially in government security jobs, you mean?"

"Yes. Particularly when there have been three murders on his patch in little more than a year."

"Black marks on the dossier?"

"And a subtle hint that three men and two young lads might all have been in the best of health just now if he'd done his job properly—whether true or false—doesn't help."

Brant kept his eyes on the road, but he asked: "Is this true, Chief?"

"It's all fixed," said Masters. "For the first of June."

"You what?" asked Green, astounded.

"It's our different way of doing things," explained Masters. "While you were trying to do Toinquet down, I was trying to fix up something positive for Brant. I think you prepared the ground and I sowed the seed. Anyhow, it appears we both succeeded."

"Oh, yes?" said Green. "Well remember, young Brant, there

are two guards there who threatened me yesterday. Your first job will be to give them the old heave-ho! Your second ..."

"He won't have much time for that sort of thing," said Hill. "Not if he's a newly married man by then."

"And newly promoted," added Masters.

Green grunted disgustedly and helped himself to a bent cigarette.

THE PERENNIAL LIBRARY MYSTERY SERIES

Delano Ames

CORPSE DIPLOMATIQUE   P 637, $2.84
"Sprightly and intelligent."

—*New York Herald Tribune Book Review*

FOR OLD CRIME'S SAKE   P 629, $2.84

MURDER, MAESTRO, PLEASE   P 630, $2.84
"If there is a more engaging couple in modern fiction than Jane and
Dagobert Brown, we have not met them."   —*Scotsman*

SHE SHALL HAVE MURDER   P 638, $2.84
"Combines the merit of both the English and American schools in the
new mystery. It's as breezy as the best of the American ones, and has
the sophistication and wit of any top-notch Britisher."

—*New York Herald Tribune Book Review*

E. C. Bentley

TRENT'S LAST CASE   P 440, $2.50
"One of the three best detective stories ever written."

—Agatha Christie

TRENT'S OWN CASE   P 516, $2.25
"I won't waste time saying that the plot is sound and the detection
satisfying. Trent has not altered a scrap and reappears with all his old
humor and charm."   —Dorothy L. Sayers

Gavin Black

A DRAGON FOR CHRISTMAS   P 473, $1.95
"Potent excitement!"   —*New York Herald Tribune*

THE EYES AROUND ME   P 485, $1.95
"I stayed up until all hours last night reading *The Eyes Around Me*,
which is something I do not do very often, but I was so intrigued by the
ingeniousness of Mr. Black's plotting and the witty way in which he spins
his mystery. I can only say that I enjoyed the book enormously."

—F. van Wyck Mason

YOU WANT TO DIE, JOHNNY?   P 472, $1.95
"Gavin Black doesn't just develop a pressure plot in suspense, he adds
uninfected wit, character, charm, and sharp knowledge of the Far East
to make rereading as keen as the first race-through."   —*Book Week*

Nicholas Blake

THE CORPSE IN THE SNOWMAN P 427, $1.95
"If there is a distinction between the novel and the detective story (which we do not admit), then this book deserves a high place in both categories."
—*The New York Times*

THE DREADFUL HOLLOW P 493, $1.95
"Pace unhurried, characters excellent, reasoning solid."
—*San Francisco Chronicle*

END OF CHAPTER P 397, $1.95
". . . admirably solid . . . an adroit formal detective puzzle backed up by firm characterization and a knowing picture of London publishing."
—*The New York Times*

HEAD OF A TRAVELER P 398, $2.25
"Another grade A detective story of the right old jigsaw persuasion."
—*New York Herald Tribune Book Review*

MINUTE FOR MURDER P 419, $1.95
"An outstanding mystery novel. Mr. Blake's writing is a delight in itself."
—*The New York Times*

THE MORNING AFTER DEATH P 520, $1.95
"One of Blake's best."
—Rex Warner

A PENKNIFE IN MY HEART P 521, $2.25
"Style brilliant . . . and suspenseful." —*San Francisco Chronicle*

THE PRIVATE WOUND P 531, $2.25
[Blake's] best novel in a dozen years . . . . An intensely penetrating study of sexual passion. . . . A powerful story of murder and its aftermath."
—Anthony Boucher, *The New York Times*

A QUESTION OF PROOF P 494, $1.95
"The characters in this story are unusually well drawn, and the suspense is well sustained."
—*The New York Times*

THE SAD VARIETY P 495, $2.25
"It is a stunner. I read it instead of eating, instead of sleeping."
—Dorothy Salisbury Davis

THERE'S TROUBLE BREWING P 569, $3.37
"Nigel Strangeways is a puzzling mixture of simplicity and penetration, but all the more real for that." —*The Times Literary Supplement*

Nicholas Blake (cont'd)

THOU SHELL OF DEATH   P 428, $1.95

"It has all the virtues of culture, intelligence and sensibility that the most exacting connoisseur could ask of detective fiction."

—*The Times* [London] *Literary Supplement*

THE WIDOW'S CRUISE   P 399, $2.25

"A stirring suspense. . . . The thrilling tale leaves nothing to be desired."

—*Springfield Republican*

THE WORM OF DEATH   P 400, $2.25

"It [The Worm of Death] is one of Blake's very best—and his best is better than almost anyone's."   —Louis Untermeyer

John & Emery Bonett

A BANNER FOR PEGASUS   P 554, $2.40

"A gem! Beautifully plotted and set. . . . Not only is the murder adroit and deserved, and the detection competent, but the love story is charming."   —Jacques Barzun and Wendell Hertig Taylor

DEAD LION   P 563, $2.40

"A clever plot, authentic background and interesting characters highly recommended this one."   —*New Republic*

Christianna Brand

GREEN FOR DANGER   P 551, $2.50

"You have to reach for the greatest of Great Names (Christie, Carr, Queen . . .) to find Brand's rivals in the devious subtleties of the trade."

—Anthony Boucher

TOUR DE FORCE   P 572, $2.40

"Complete with traps for the over-ingenious, a double-reverse surprise ending and a key clue planted so fairly and obviously that you completely overlook it. If that's your idea of perfect entertainment, then seize at once upon *Tour de Force.*"   —Anthony Boucher, *The New York Times*

James Byrom

OR BE HE DEAD   P 585, $2.84

"A very original tale . . . Well written and steadily entertaining."

—Jacques Barzun & Wendell Hertig Taylor, *A Catalogue of Crime*

Henry Calvin

IT'S DIFFERENT ABROAD   P 640, $2.84
"What is remarkable and delightful, Mr. Calvin imparts a flavor of satire
to what he renovates and compels us to take straight."

—Jacques Barzun

Marjorie Carleton

VANISHED   P 559, $2.40
"Exceptional . . . a minor triumph."
—Jacques Barzun and Wendell Hertig Taylor, *A Catalogue of Crime*

George Harmon Coxe

MURDER WITH PICTURES   P 527, $2.25
"[Coxe] has hit the bull's-eye with his first shot."

—*The New York Times*

Edmund Crispin

BURIED FOR PLEASURE   P 506, $2.50
"Absolute and unalloyed delight."

—Anthony Boucher, *The New York Times*

Lionel Davidson

THE MENORAH MEN   P 592, $2.84
"Of his fellow thriller writers, only John Le Carré shows the same
instinct for the viscera."   —*Chicago Tribune*

NIGHT OF WENCESLAS   P 595, $2.84
"A most ingenious thriller, so enriched with style, wit, and a sense of
serious comedy that it all but transcends its kind."

—*The New Yorker*

THE ROSE OF TIBET   P 593, $2.84
"I hadn't realized how much I missed the genuine Adventure story
. . . until I read *The Rose of Tibet*."   —Graham Greene

D. M. Devine

MY BROTHER'S KILLER   P 558, $2.40
"A most enjoyable crime story which I enjoyed reading down to the last
moment."   —Agatha Christie

Kenneth Fearing

THE BIG CLOCK P 500, $1.95

"It will be some time before chill-hungry clients meet again so rare a compound of irony, satire, and icy-fingered narrative. *The Big Clock* is . . . a psychothriller you won't put down." —*Weekly Book Review*

Andrew Garve

THE ASHES OF LODA P 430, $1.50

"Garve . . . embellishes a fine fast adventure story with a more credible picture of the U.S.S.R. than is offered in most thrillers."
—*The New York Times Book Review*

THE CUCKOO LINE AFFAIR P 451, $1.95

". . . an agreeable and ingenious piece of work." —*The New Yorker*

A HERO FOR LEANDA P 429, $1.50

"One can trust Mr. Garve to put a fresh twist to any situation, and the ending is really a lovely surprise." —*The Manchester Guardian*

MURDER THROUGH THE LOOKING GLASS P 449, $1.95

". . . refreshingly out-of-the-way and enjoyable . . . highly recommended to all comers." —*Saturday Review*

NO TEARS FOR HILDA P 441, $1.95

"It starts fine and finishes finer. I got behind on breathing watching Max get not only his man but his woman, too." —Rex Stout

THE RIDDLE OF SAMSON P 450, $1.95

"The story is an excellent one, the people are quite likable, and the writing is superior." —*Springfield Republican*

Michael Gilbert

BLOOD AND JUDGMENT P 446, $1.95

"Gilbert readers need scarcely be told that the characters all come alive at first sight, and that his surpassing talent for narration enhances any plot. . . . Don't miss." —*San Francisco Chronicle*

THE BODY OF A GIRL P 459, $1.95

"Does what a good mystery should do: open up into all kinds of ramifications, with untold menace behind the action. At the end, there is a bang-up climax, and it is a pleasure to see how skilfully Gilbert wraps everything up." —*The New York Times Book Review*

DEATH WALKS THE WOODS P 556, $2.40

"Here is a fine formal detective story, with a technically brilliant solution demanding the attention of all connoisseurs of construction."

—Anthony Boucher, *The New York Times Book Review*

AN ENGLISH MURDER P 455, $2.50

"By a long shot, the best crime story I have read for a long time. Everything is traditional, but originality does not suffer. The setting is perfect. Full marks to Mr. Hare." —*Irish Press*

SUICIDE EXCEPTED P 636, $2.84

"Adroit in its manipulation . . . and distinguished by a plot-twister which I'll wager Christie wishes she'd thought of."

—*The New York Times*

TENANT FOR DEATH P 570, $2.84

"The way in which an air of probability is combined both with clear, terse narrative and with a good deal of subtle suburban atmosphere, proves the extreme skill of the writer." —*The Spectator*

TRAGEDY AT LAW P 522, $2.25

"An extremely urbane and well-written detective story."

—*The New York Times*

UNTIMELY DEATH P 514, $2.25

"The English detective story at its quiet best, meticulously underplayed, rich in perceivings of the droll human animal and ready at the last with a neat surprise which has been there all the while had we but wits to see it." —*New York Herald Tribune Book Review*

THE WIND BLOWS DEATH P 589, $2.84

"A plot compounded of musical knowledge, a Dickens allusion, and a subtle point in law is related with delightfully unobtrusive wit, warmth, and style." —*The New York Times*

WITH A BARE BODKIN P 523, $2.25

"One of the best detective stories published for a long time."

—*The Spectator*

Robert Harling

THE ENORMOUS SHADOW P 545, $2.50

"In some ways the best spy story of the modern period. . . . The writing is terse and vivid . . . the ending full of action . . . altogether first-rate."

—Jacques Barzun and Wendell Hertig Taylor, *A Catalogue of Crime*

Matthew Head

THE CABINDA AFFAIR   P 541, $2.25
"An absorbing whodunit and a distinguished novel of atmosphere."
                          —Anthony Boucher, *The New York Times*

THE CONGO VENUS   P 597, $2.84
"Terrific. The dialogue is just plain wonderful."
                                        —*The Boston Globe*

MURDER AT THE FLEA CLUB   P 542, $2.50
"The true delight is in Head's style, its limpid ease combined with humor
and an awesome precision of phrase."   —*San Francisco Chronicle*

M. V. Heberden

ENGAGED TO MURDER   P 533, $2.25
"Smooth plotting."   —*The New York Times*

James Hilton

WAS IT MURDER?   P 501, $1.95
"The story is well planned and well written."
                                        —*The New York Times*

P. M. Hubbard

HIGH TIDE   P 571, $2.40
"A smooth elaboration of mounting horror and danger."
                                        —*Library Journal*

Elspeth Huxley

THE AFRICAN POISON MURDERS   P 540, $2.25
"Obscure venom, manical mutilations, deadly bush fire, thrilling climax
compose major opus.... Top-flight."
                                 —*Saturday Review of Literature*

MURDER ON SAFARI   P 587, $2.84
"Right now we'd call Mrs. Huxley a dangerous rival to Agatha Christie."   —*Books*

Francis Iles

BEFORE THE FACT   P 517, $2.50

"Not many 'serious' novelists have produced character studies to compare with Iles's internally terrifying portrait of the murderer in *Before the Fact,* his masterpiece and a work truly deserving the appellation of unique and beyond price."   —Howard Haycraft

MALICE AFORETHOUGHT   P 532, $1.95

"It is a long time since I have read anything so good as *Malice Aforethought,* with its cynical humour, acute criminology, plausible detail and rapid movement. It makes you hug yourself with pleasure."
                                      —H. C. Harwood, *Saturday Review*

Michael Innes

THE CASE OF THE JOURNEYING BOY   P 632, $3.12

"I could see no faults in it. There is no one to compare with him."
                                         —*Illustrated London News*

DEATH BY WATER   P 574, $2.40

"The amount of ironic social criticism and deft characterization of scenes and people would serve another author for six books."
                              —Jacques Barzun and Wendell Hertig Taylor

HARE SITTING UP   P 590, $2.84

"There is hardly anyone (in mysteries or mainstream) more exquisitely literate, allusive and Jamesian—and hardly anyone with a firmer sense of melodramatic plot or a more vigorous gift of storytelling."
                                —Anthony Boucher, *The New York Times*

THE LONG FAREWELL   P 575, $2.40

"A model of the deft, classic detective story, told in the most wittily diverting prose."   —*The New York Times*

THE MAN FROM THE SEA   P 591, $2.84

"The pace is brisk, the adventures exciting and excitingly told, and above all he keeps to the very end the interesting ambiguity of the man from the sea."   —*New Statesman*

THE SECRET VANGUARD   P 584, $2.84

"Innes . . . has mastered the art of swift, exciting and well-organized narrative."   —*The New York Times*

THE WEIGHT OF THE EVIDENCE   P 633, $2.84

"First-class puzzle, deftly solved. University background interesting and amusing."   —*Saturday Review of Literature*

Mary Kelly

THE SPOILT KILL   P 565, $2.40

"Mary Kelly is a new Dorothy Sayers. . . . [An] exciting new novel."
                                              —*Evening News*

Lange Lewis

THE BIRTHDAY MURDER   P 518, $1.95

"Almost perfect in its playlike purity and delightful prose."
                        —Jacques Barzun and Wendell Hertig Taylor

Allan MacKinnon

HOUSE OF DARKNESS   P 582, $2.84

"His best . . . a perfect compendium."
        —Jacques Barzun & Wendell Hertig Taylor, *A Catalogue of Crime*

Arthur Maling

LUCKY DEVIL   P 482, $1.95

"The plot unravels at a fast clip, the writing is breezy and Maling's
approach is as fresh as today's stockmarket quotes."
                                  —*Louisville Courier Journal*

RIPOFF   P 483, $1.95

"A swiftly paced story of today's big business is larded with intrigue as
a Ralph Nader-type investigates an insurance scandal and is soon on the
run from a hired gun and his brother. . . . Engrossing and credible."
                                              —*Booklist*

SCHROEDER'S GAME   P 484, $1.95

"As the title indicates, this Schroeder is up to something, and the un-
ravelling of his game is a diverting and sufficiently blood-soaked entertainment."   —*The New Yorker*

Austin Ripley

MINUTE MYSTERIES   P 387, $2.50

More than one hundred of the world's shortest detective stories. Only
one possible solution to each case!

Thomas Sterling

THE EVIL OF THE DAY   P 529, $2.50

"Prose as witty and subtle as it is sharp and clear. . .characters unconven-
tionally conceived and richly bodied forth . . . . In short, a novel to be
treasured."   —Anthony Boucher, *The New York Times*

Julian Symons

THE BELTING INHERITANCE   P 468, $1.95
"A superb whodunit in the best tradition of the detective story."
     —August Derleth, *Madison Capital Times*

BLAND BEGINNING   P 469, $1.95
"Mr. Symons displays a deft storytelling skill, a quiet and literate wit, a nice feeling for character, and detectival ingenuity of a high order."
     —Anthony Boucher, *The New York Times*

BOGUE'S FORTUNE   P 481, $1.95
"There's a touch of the old sardonic humour, and more than a touch of style."   —*The Spectator*

THE BROKEN PENNY   P 480, $1.95
"The most exciting, astonishing and believable spy story to appear in years.   —Anthony Boucher, *The New York Times Book Review*

THE COLOR OF MURDER   P 461, $1.95
"A singularly unostentatious and memorably brilliant detective story."
     —*New York Herald Tribune Book Review*

Dorothy Stockbridge Tillet
(John Stephen Strange)

THE MAN WHO KILLED FORTESCUE   P 536, $2.25
"Better than average."   —*Saturday Review of Literature*

Simon Troy

THE ROAD TO RHUINE   P 583, $2.84
"Unusual and agreeably told."   —*San Francisco Chronicle*

SWIFT TO ITS CLOSE   P 546, $2.40
"A nicely literate British mystery . . . the atmosphere and the plot are exceptionally well wrought, the dialogue excellent."   —*Best Sellers*

Henry Wade

THE DUKE OF YORK'S STEPS   P 588, $2.84
"A classic of the golden age."
     —Jacques Barzun & Wendell Hertig Taylor, *A Catalogue of Crime*

A DYING FALL   P 543, $2.50
"One of those expert British suspense jobs . . . it crackles with undercurrents of blackmail, violent passion and murder. Topnotch in its class."
     —*Time*

Henry Wade (cont'd)

THE HANGING CAPTAIN   P 548, $2.50

"This is a detective story for connoisseurs, for those who value clear thinking and good writing above mere ingenuity and easy thrills."

—*Times Literary Supplement*

Hillary Waugh

LAST SEEN WEARING . . .   P 552, $2.40

"A brilliant tour de force."   —Julian Symons

THE MISSING MAN   P 553, $2.40

"The quiet detailed police work of Chief Fred C. Fellows, Stockford, Conn., is at its best in *The Missing Man* . . . one of the Chief's toughest cases and one of the best handled."

—Anthony Boucher, *The New York Times Book Review*

Henry Kitchell Webster

WHO IS THE NEXT?   P 539, $2.25

"A double murder, private-plane piloting, a neat impersonation, and a delicate courtship are adroitly combined by a writer who knows how to use the language."   —Jacques Barzun and Wendell Hertig Taylor

Anna Mary Wells

MURDERER'S CHOICE   P 534, $2.50

"Good writing, ample action, and excellent character work."

—*Saturday Review of Literature*

A TALENT FOR MURDER   P 535, $2.25

"The discovery of the villain is a decided shock."   —*Books*

Edward Young

THE FIFTH PASSENGER   P 544, $2.25

"Clever and adroit . . . excellent thriller . . ."   —*Library Journal*

If you enjoyed this book you'll want to know about
THE PERENNIAL LIBRARY MYSTERY SERIES

Buy them at your local bookstore or use this coupon for ordering:

Qty	P number	Price
————	————	————
————	————	————
————	————	————
————	————	————
————	————	————
————	————	————
————	————	————
————	————	————
————	————	————
————	————	————
————	————	————
————	————	————
————	————	————
————	————	————

postage and handling charge $1.00
———— book(s) @ $0.25

TOTAL [————]

**Prices contained in this coupon are Harper & Row invoice prices only.
They are subject to change without notice, and in no way reflect the prices at
which these books may be sold by other suppliers.**

**HARPER & ROW, Mail Order Dept. #PMS, 10 East 53rd St., New
York, N.Y. 10022.**

Please send me the books I have checked above. I am enclosing $————
which includes a postage and handling charge of $1.00 for the first book and
25¢ for each additional book. Send check or money order. No cash or
C.O.D.s please

Name————————————————————————

Address——————————————————————

City———————— State———— Zip————
Please allow 4 weeks for delivery. USA only. This offer expires 2/28/85.
Please add applicable sales tax.